FROM CUBA WITH A SONG

SEVERO SARDUY

FROM CUBA

with a song

Translated from the Spanish
by Suzanne Jill Levine

LOS ANGELES • SUN & MOON PRESS
1994

Sun & Moon Press
A Program of The Contemporary Arts Educational Project, Inc.
a nonprofit corporation
6026 Wilshire Boulevard, Los Angeles, California 90036

This edition first published in paperback in 1994 by Sun & Moon Press
10 9 8 7 6 5 4 3 2 1
FIRST ENGLISH LANGUAGE PAPERBACK EDITION
©1967 by Severo Sarduy
Reprinted by permission
Published originally as *De donde son los cantantes*
by Joaquín Mortiz, Mexico, 1967
Translation ©1994, 1972 by Suzanne Jill Levine

This book was made possible, in part, through an operational grant from
the Andrew W. Mellon Foundation, through a grant from
The National Endowment for the Arts, a nonprofit corporation, and
through contributions to The Contemporary Arts Educational Project, Inc.,
a nonprofit corporation

Cover: Lydia Rubio, *Beba Suarez, Looking at a Landscape*
Reprinted by permission of the artist
Cover Design: Katie Messborn
Typography: Guy Bennett

LIBRARY OF CONGRESS CATALOGING IN PUBLICATION DATA
Sarduy, Severo [1937–1993]
[De donde son los cantantes. English]
From Cuba with a Song / Severo Sarduy; translated from the
Spanish by Suzanne Jill Levine, —1st English language pbk. ed.
p. cm — (Sun & Moon Classics: 52)
ISBN: 1-55713-158-9 : $10.95
I. Levine, Suzanne Jill. II. Title.
PQ7390.S28D413 1994
863—dc20
94-28405
CIP

Printed in the United States of America on acid-free paper.

To Salamandra

TRANSLATOR'S NOTE

From Cuba with a Song—literally "from where are the singers," words from a traditional Cuban song or *son*—can be summarized, if you wish, as a parody of Cuban history, in which Cuba's racial diversity is represented fantasmagorically by three components: Chinese, African, Spanish. Sarduy's physical features seemed a hybrid of all three, though his ancestor from Macao is by far the most remote source; he found something of himself in the Asian worldview, and was as a youth captivated by the metamorphic charms of Havana's Chinatown, fixed here in a witty, nostalgic portrayal. Obviously this version of history is a parodical reduction since other ethnicities—notably the decimated indigenous groups such as the Taìnos—are not represented. Sarduy's point may be that all texts are versions, never the thing itself, and more importantly, that history is written by the white conqueror. But rather than reduce the irreducible (and Sarduy himself does it as eloquently as it can be done in his "Note" at the end of this brief novel), I would like simply to clarify that this edition is a revised translation by me, over twenty years after the first edition. I had the good fortune back then, in 1971, to be assisted in this "impossible task" by the author as well as by scholars such as Emir Rodrìguez Monegal and Roberto Gonzàlez Echevarrìa, and have discussed this translation at length in a book called *The Subversive Scribe,* explaining, among other things, how the title came about. Suffice it to say here that revising the translation has been a very positive experience, not only catching finally those errata that had been annoying me all this time, but having a second chance to refine and polish, to use a rather well-worn metaphor. Language is always metaphor, Sarduy's writing tells us, hence infinitely slippery. A writer's work is never done, Borges said more than once; at some point it just gets published. And then it's the reader's turn.

Suzanne Jill Levine

FROM CUBA WITH A SONG

Feathers, yes, lovely brimstone feathers, heads of marble carried down a river of feathers, feathers on her head, a feather, hummingbird, and raspberry hat in fact, from which Help's smooth orange nylon hair stretches to the ground, braided with pink ribbons and little bells; from her hat the albino locks cascade down the sides of her face, then hips, down her zebra-skin boots to the pavement. And Help, in stripes, an Indian bird behind falling rain.

"I can't go on!"—she shrieks, and carves a hole in the bread crumbs.

"Drop dead!"—Mercy speaking—"Yeah, drop dead, stick with it, kill yourself, go tell the president, go tell the gods, shove it, split into two like an orange, drown in beer, in franks and sauerkraut, fuck yourself. Turn to dust, to ashes. That's what you wanted."

Help pushes aside her locks. She peeps out, Baroque:

> "I will be ashes, but meaningful ashes.
> I will be dust, but dust in love."

MERCY: *Tu me casses les cothurnes! (en français dans le texte).*
Shut up. I can't go on either. Wipe away that tear. A
little modesty, please. And poise. Stick with it. Take
your compact.

The small mirror is signaling. It directs the sun toward
the glass skyscraper. On the balcony of the twentieth floor
a girl comes out with another mirror in her hand. She
hops up and down and moves it around in search of the
call.

"Look at yourself. Your tears have made a furrow in
the first five layers of your makeup. Make sure they don't
reach your skin. Of course for that you'd need a drill.
You've lost the asparagus cream. The underlying strawberry is mixing with the layer of Max Factor's baby pineapple. You're graph-papered. Vasarelic. Let's sing:

> the ever-absent, ever absent
> gives us evil as a present."

Help, almost singing:

"Yes, that's him. The riddle of riddles. The sixty-four
thousand dollar question, the definition of being. Our
cupboard's empty. No ham for Tom. No cheese for Jerry.
This is how it stands: we stayed behind and the gods went
away, they took the boat, they left in trucks, they crossed
the border, they shat on the Pyrenees. They've all gone.
This is how it stands: we went away and the gods stayed
behind. Sitting. Hiding, taking a nap, happy-go-lucky,
dancing the Ma Teodora, The First Cuban Song, the repetitive *son,* swinging in midair, like strung-up corpses."

"Shut up. That's what you wanted."

"No. I didn't want this. I asked for life, all of it, with the rattles and the tambourines. I asked for my daily bread and sausage. No go. They sent me the hairless old woman, the plucked, bald, shaven, lonely bitch of death."

"One of your cheeks is showing. It's like the face of the moon: full of craters."

"Rat. Rogue. Frog. May the Being swallow you. Inhale you. May your air conditioning break down. May a hole open all around you. May the Lacanian fault suck you under. May you be absorbed, not seen because unnoticed."

"That's it. I'm leaving. I mean it now. No matter how. They're throwing me out. I'm cornered and with my lance I strike right and left, to and fro, like a Japanese warrior fighting an invisible enemy."

Help moves her head. Golden fringes against the windowpane. Woolen locks. Windmill wings.

"Go away. Unessential. Leave the House. Yes, house with capitals. The Domus Dei." And she nods the way.

MERCY IN THE DOMUS DEI

But how could you not be confused? There were thousands. Thousands of little feet. Little worm-eaten hands. Such screeching. Tin plates and spoons. They'd come out looking green and charge against the waves. Siren, and they'd appear. Screeching, and they'd disappear. At the same time. A woman would go to each window. And at each, shake a black tablecloth. The front of the building would disappear behind a curtain of bread crumbs. River of feathers.

"Good morning. I've been phoning and nobody answers."

"Ah," the maid says.

"May I come in?"

"Won't do you any good. She's not in."

"What? After all the time. All the waiting. All the bootlicking and backslapping. I've gone down on my knees in waiting rooms, bounced between the sheets of every minister, bribed doormen."

"Sorry, no."

The maid opens the door wide, as if she were opening her legs, her transparent little box, to the being par excellence. A light erupts from inside: the light reflected from the bald pate of the Great Bald Madame. Mercy contracts all over, turns white, like squid in boiling water.

"Now do you see?"—the acolyte utters hoarsely—"She's conspicuous for her absence."

By the time Mercy's on the elevator, poor thing, she's screaming at the top of her lungs. A crying little frog face. She mixes up her buttons, bumps against a black man, catches her finger in the door. And so she reaches the ground floor: moaning, bishop purple, cowering in a corner of the aluminum box, surrounded by plucked chickens on all sides, alone with them except for a block of crushed ice and a shopping bag of bitter oranges in one corner.

You ought to hear the cute words the midget doorman saves for lady visitors! He comes out from under his scarlet cap and exhausts the synonymies. With Mercy it's a different story; frozen and all as she is, she kicks him at the first flattery, ties him to the stool with his own belt, presses the button to the roof-garden and launches the echo chamber.

There are mirrors in the hall, and, although threadbare, the Fate just can't stand herself: she pulls out her hogs bristle brush, her orange, diamond-studded eye shadow, the false beauty mark that she places painstakingly on the right corner of her lips so that it rises with each smile, lastly she pulls out her Yoruba necklaces and when she steps out on the street she is something else. To such a point that Help, waiting for her with coupon in hand—good for two mango milk shakes at the Milk Bar on the corner—jumps with joy upon seeing her and waves a handkerchief: she thinks Mercy was received.

"No, I wasn't."

When they turn, slender and symmetrical, toward the building, the windows are already dark. There is no noise. The bread crumbs have bleached the treetops, the black lawn.

"It's like snow!"

SELF-SERVICE

"My, we're metaphysical, we must be hungry! Let's go to the Self-Service!"

No sooner said than done. They're off on tiptoes, pressing their tummies, slipping among the shells of rusty cars—their silky hair flows through tin scraps—stumbling, jumping over flattened and spokeless bicycle wheels, over handlebars, moss-covered horns, headlights stuffed with paper, aluminum circles with red bars. Yellow deities.

Flavian birds. Stags. They walk among glass, girdled by rain, crowned with frozen orchids from Palm Beach, clean among the dregs, clear-cut as mushrooms upon horse dung, fragrant among the debris of diesel motors.

Following the scaffolds of a construction site—in the foundations, puddles of green water—they walk along singing *Ich bin von Kopf bis Fuss auf Liebe eingestellt,* opening their hungry little fish mouths into heartshapes, tightrope walking on a steel bar.

And behind them, thousands of paper balloons simultaneously light up within squares. Cones upon a red tapestry. And over the buildings, the milky wake of the subway streaks the night. Intermittent blue rhombi.

And off they go, the Flower Girls, the Ever-Present cross another scaffold, another avenue. There they go, under the three-leaf clover of the highways watched by helicopters. Echo tunnels. There, by the escalators, by the rails, where all the trolleys are, a second before the go signal. How speedy!

One potato, two potato, one by one they pick up the potatoes under the table, crouching among feet; she crawls along the gallery of legs, behind a rolling tomato, the paper cup, the bowl of grated beets—little purple strands on somebody's shoe.

People jump over her. Down there, on all fours, entangled in her own wig, soup-soaked Help has fallen with her plate among open tangerines (a spiked heel perforates her jellied egg).

She picks it all up—dirty home fried potatoes—looking up from side to side like a frightened squirrel. She puts on her green glasses. Covers the other half of her face with bangs.

"I want to disappear!"—and she's no longer a squirrel, but a mole: she rolls herself into a ball, and hides her head.

Mercy is now seated, but not eating. She's looking at the food and sobbing rhythmically. She boohoos and blows her nose with a Kleenex. When Help arrives empty-handed—she threw her plate into the garbage can—she shakes her by the shoulders.

"It's nothing," she says.

"It's nothing," she answers.

And they laugh again.

Now both are seated, calm and collected, in front of a celluloid picture window. Not one stain, not one hair out of place, not one drop of tomato sauce on their cheeks. Motionless, their heads, a few inches apart, coincide with the crossing of the diagonal lines in the landscape—blue domes punctured with windows, an airfield: drones and twin engines are taking off—pale hands on their chests. They don't move an inch, but it's useless: everybody's looking at them. They feel on trial.

"Mocking eyes give us the once-over."

"Fingers point to us, put asterisks on us."

Then Help puts her finger to her right temple, jumps up, shaking her mane like a feather duster, clinking her little bells; the girl's all music.

"I have an idea."

She opens a crocodile-skin box that hangs from her shoulder like a canteen on a thin silver chain, and counting them she takes out fifty color photographs. She throws away two which have yellowed, hands Mercy a close-up

in black and white, and goes to the end of the dining room
with the other forty-seven. From there she starts handing
them out, table by table. With each photograph she smiles,
combs her hair, introduces herself to the addressee with a
bow and doubles his surprise with a detailed description
of the picture. Mercy follows her a few steps behind, adding adverbs to the adjectives, curtsies to the bows, cooling the air with an ostrich feather fan, spraying it with
balms. At Help's signal, Mercy gives each a little Caridad
del Cobre* medallion and a piece of candy.

The first picture is already faded. Help, with her face
painted yellow, is in a guayabera shirt and cap, drinking
coffee in front of a cardboard tower, or a Mardi Gras float,
or a mausoleum lettered in Arabic.

"Here I am in front of the blue mosque of Constan-
tinople, even though you can't see the four turrets. The
suit is Empress Ming's, that's why I have that dragon-
painted teacup in one hand and this single-flowered long
stem in the other. As you see, my eyes are elongated by
means of black lines which, in profile, if it weren't for my
ears, would turn into little fishes."

"You forgot to say that these sniveling, bare-assed little
boys who are playing mandolins, mouths agape before
the lens, are your interpreters."

"My followers. Look at this one. Here I am among the
Caduvean or Cadivean Indians, reading Franz Boas with
a tape recorder. What the native is handing me is a mask
whose general lines correspond to the map of the city. I
look good, don't I?"

* The Virgin of the Caridad del Cobre—the patron saint of Cuba.

And thus, she hands out all the pictures. Except one. She keeps the passport size six by eight, in which she is face front, looking slightly to one side, not really serious, in short, her spitting image.

"I don't think we left a bad impression."

"Maybe. But let's go before they change their minds."

"Wait. I forgot my scythe."

Note: The Self-Service is on the ground floor of a Bakelite octahedron. Walls of Coca Cola bottles support a ceiling decorated by a Fall of Icarus in pale pink and gold. From the corners four spotlights move sinusoidally along the walls and sometimes stop on bowls of grated carrots, jellied eggs, or red beets in almond sauce which are imbedded in wicker nooks between the bottles. At each sweep of the light a xylophone arpeggio ascends or descends in the scale according to the altitude of the light beam, and stops on a note when the beam stops on a plate. Since the red beets in almond sauce are practically at ceiling level, the corresponding note is a shriek that turns hoarse when the focus descends in the sinusoid.

The delicacies, like the plates which contain them, are made of plastic.

A New Version of the Facts: Fate and the General

If she entangled him in her champagne locks, if he pricked her with the open brooch of one of his medals, if the cherry tart fell on the Carmelite khaki of his uniform, if he scratched her with a gold braid, if both got entangled, if they held their tongues out of courtesy, if they insulted each other, if the creamed asparagus remained among the decorations of honor, if the Pyrrhic victor invoked the patron saint of artillerymen, the invincible goddess Changó, if she retorted by calling upon the queen of the river and the sky, her antidote and talisman: we will never know.

Let's make a note then on how it stands at this moment: facing the dessert department, among synovial trays and trembling like a burnt butterfly, Help has entangled her hairs…No: her hairs are tangled in the aluminum forest that armors a skinny general of the fleet.

There they are—two plumed serpents—cheek to cheek, stuck to one another, their trays stuck together too. Struggling Siamese twins. Bacardí bat, ink spot, double animal, open oyster, a body with its reflection; that's Help and the General.

There they stay, touching at their vertices, extremes meeting. Like a rattlesnake that finds a jiggling, appetizing little mouthful for itself, a pyramidal cupcake that it downs in one gulp, letting loose the scream then, because it's just downed its own tail, and thus disappears and returns to Bald Nothingness.

"But why doesn't the General simply take off his coat?"

Listen to the question that Mercy, and only Mercy, asks.

I: My dear, can't you see that if the General takes off his hardwares, he would be like Lacan's bird painter without his feathers? Like a goat who takes off his black stripes to create a Vasarely with them?

MERCY: I just want Help out of this mess, that's all.

I: She'll get out. She'll go home well-mannered, conceited, chaste.

MERCY: Listen to that! Three adjectives in one breath! It wasn't like that in my day. What today's literature is coming to…

I: Yes dearie, three adjectives in a row, but well put. So shut your mouth and swallow.

MERCY: Digressions are not my line, so to the point: what's happened to my friend?

Nothing really, just that this cosmogony-in-the-making simply attracted, sucked in world. As a magnet in a river does to fishhooks, or as a vacuum cleaner in a chicken coop to feathers, so did the binomial Help-General suck in all that was around, and naturally, a black girl and Chinese chick: thus completing the curriculum cubense.

As always, the fourth element, that is, the Unnamable Baldy, was already present. It was stuck on to the third which is always hero-worshipped for its strength, well then, the two that were missing came running. They arrived, twin stones, fish of identical eyes, to get caught in the hair and medals, to entangle themselves in Help Conception of the Universe:

1. an oriental, in white rice powder makeup, prima donna of the Shanghai District Opera,

2. a round-assed, big-titted black girl, very semicircular, very double-breasted, snuggly squeezed into a bright red weave, her hair freshly ironed like a river of creeping vines.

So that, seen from above, in an imaginary mirror which we can place on top of the self-service counter for example (and which is probably there, to see if someone is taking the silverware or hiding, as he passes, a chocolate cookie in his pocket), the group is a giant four-leaf clover, or a four-headed animal facing the four cardinal points, or a Yoruba sign of the four roads:

the white of the wig and the coat,

the China doll of the lottery and the mouth cat cabala

the Wifredo Lamesque black girl

and the last—who was the first:

the red-headed fraud, the Waxen Woman, the Keep-Your-Fingers-Crossed Loner. We come upon them, the four parts of which the wise stud of Heidelberg speaks.

MERCY: Yeah, the one who put the lid on the box.

They're all yours now. Four different beings and four who are one. Already they're breaking loose, already they're looking at each other. How cute!

BY THE RIVER OF ROSE ASHES

In the forest of Havana
a Chinee lost her way
and I, a poor lost goner,
this fair maid did waylay.
　　—HOMAGE TO THE "SHANGHAI,"
　　　HAVANA BURLESQUE

The moon, the partridge, the fading ferns, the four animals, the wine of the wind, the water of the Almendares: all was set for the rendezvous.

There, among the trunks of violet-striped sugar cane, licking reeds, following the crease of leaves like knives, silvery drivel, the snake jiggled its rattles along with the river's.

And nearby, the red turtle, the one that runs fastest: saddle of the immortals.

Further away, eyes of fire among the black leaves of the royal poinciana, the unicorn, with its hemplike mane. And next to him, the forever-on-one-foot, the pink heron.

The earth's murmur was like the clashing of sticks in The Capture of an Enemy Fort, so it wasn't at all strange to see Rose Ashes there. Sewn into that landscape, exercising her Yin right smack in the forest of Havana, she was a white bird behind bamboo, a motionless prisoner among lances. She was reciting the Five Books, singing with her little whistle voice; she looked as if she'd burst like a salty toad; she'd gaze at the moon in silence and recite them over again.

So did the sweet smoke of the Romeo and Juliet, Havana's finest cigar, and clanking medals surprise her.

She did not turn pale; she already was, from so much rice and tea.

Whether she was dressed to receive ambassadors from the provinces in the Garden of Ming; or wearing black slacks and a linen guayabera, as usual, or plain and simply in the state her mother, with one good push, bore her during intermission at the Opera, we'll never know.

Honoris Causa in pool and in the sack—those were her battlefields—the Condecorated, the Glorious One, did thus surprise her. Cushioned by a quilt of moss he crushed sleeping scorpions and orange snails, his step was the Invincible's: pectoral golds, its punctuation. He was the hood master of Seville's processions, the majesty of synagogues, the Galician *aîdos* in forward march. Not a general, but a long-shanked gladiator, yes.

The yellow one shrieked. And with good reason. He kept coming, parting branches, dealing blows, his arms, a double machete, his air, one of combat as he fought his way through the bramble. A Peeping Tom, the licentious rake, and another mystic. But you must admit, the gymnastic arts sure come in handy! Lotus Flower leaps up, and, like the fish that jumping out of water becomes a hummingbird, she flies among lianas. Now she's the white mask striped by shadows of sugar canes, now the flight of a dove, the streak of a rabbit. Try and see her. You can't. Yes! her eyes, two golden slits, snake charmer eyes, betray her. A puckery *caimito* among clusters of *caimitos*. She's mimicry. She's a texture—the white plaques on the trunk of a God tree—a wilted flower beneath a palm, a butterfly embossed with pupils, she is pure symmetry. Where is she? I don't see her. She scarcely breathes. Now, with eyebrow pencil she draws faces on her hands and wiggles them far from her own, to bewilder Mr. Belicose. He, dividing the air with his sword, curses her in alphabetical order.

Rose Ashes becomes a cloud, a baby fawn, the murmur of the river among its pebbles. So they go around in circles, searching each other out with a stare, like two fighting cocks. And so recitation time passes.

The China maid attacks. Changes disguise, throws stones, appears and disappears in the same place, runs zigzag so that no weapon can reach her, erects a stone barrier to make the river run in the other direction and mislead the Enemy; she scats centipedes, squirrels, chameleons, so that they'll bite him as he passes; she imitates the clanking medals, the very voice of her pursuer, or appears as another lecherous general to drive him crazy. One by one she exhausts her scenic resources.

The Butcher is ready to fight. For him, her escapes are like the carriages of gold they give an invader to stop him. Around and around his prisoner he goes: it's no longer one but two swords he carries. With the second knife, the one that bends but never breaks, he opens the underbrush. A Pyrrhic little flute that one!

The finer the Yellow One becomes, the more liquid it gets, the sword you all know, the more fiery; why it's almost two-tongued!

Naturally, with an ally like that, it doesn't take long for Mr. Lecherous to attempt checkmate.

The Forest of Havana is the Summer Palace's forest, and the waters of the Almendares, the Yangtze; Rose Ashes weaves her own figure with lianas and flees, leaving her adversary with that intangible double, that unraveling and moving image.

He subtly approaches from behind; but abandoned by Chola Angüengue, the conga queen of weapons, he gets caught in her loom.

Faraway, the China maid shrieks, and dances the Canton mambo. And he, stuck, here. Still.

Do you smell something? Yes, that's the smell: Cantonese rice with soya sauce. There's something else too: dog urine (it's early); plus: tea. Yes, as you must have guessed, we're in Chinatown.

THE READER: But, what about that record of Marlene's?

I: Well, dear, not everything in life is coherent. A little disorder with the order, I always say. You're not going to ask me to arrange a full-feathered Chinese "ensemble" for you right here on Zanja Street, next to the Pacifico (yes, where Heming-way eats), in a city where there's a distillery, pool hall, whore, and sailor on every corner. I'll do what I can.

And so:

"Chinese atmosphere, girls, come on!"—the Director steps out of a saffron cloud smelling of burnt grass (yes, the same grass you're thinking). He steps out of his pagoda of smoke, pensive, hair greased with sweat, eyes of a jade bulldog—two red balls—hands crossed over his chest (is he reciting the Book?); he walks along a dotted line. He shivers, turns green; the opalescent cloud crumbles in the scenery. He is lime green, a rooster feather, he bristles; a poisonous wind has swept through his nine orifices.

He's inspired. He calmly approaches, looking toward the stage, but in *his* reality he's making his way through battles, he's escaping bats that are Toledan blades, he's crushing rows of ants and red dwarfs, he's riding on a tortoise. For us he's taking off an earring; but he's pulling leeches off his ears. Is he fanning himself with his hands? On grass level he's commanding the Waters. Is he scratching his neck? He's trying to get a gorilla off his back, or a troll who's biting his shoulder. The Director, stoned, plays on both waves; he's an amphibian of consciousness, the *mascalzone.*

He's wearing canvas pants, an orange sash at his waist, open sandals, and, above all, a little aroma I'd prefer not to evoke but which is stronger than the stench of badly digested glazed pork.

He stands on the empty proscenium, but feels looked at. He catches by surprise, between cracks in the stage, sliding, parallel drops of mercury, neon green eyes.

"A cup of coffee, mæstro!"—Comes shuffling Lotus Flower by the River of Rose Ashes, her flowered silk bathrobe opened. Through the other stage door María Eng enters, with Dragon Puss, Frog Baby and the Ever-Present Girls, better known as the Fannies: Help Chong and Mercy Si-Yuen, chorus girls of the Shanghai District Opera. The very same who perform a flying somersault through loop-holes and splash down inside the castle in The Attack on the Fort, and again, the same who come out butterflies and turn into toads among the leaves of the white water lilies in the Poem of the Barge, yep, that's them. We'll soon see them go through changes, keepers that they are of the secret of the seventy-eight metamorphoses.

To set the stage, now that we're in rehearsal, Lotus Flower sounds her note somewhere between twitched and gurgled (a flute full of beer), but as the naughty *cattiva* doesn't warn anybody in this manner, María, Dragon Puss, and the Siamese twins come running out to Chinese C.

(Outside, the neighborhood's waking up: in the brothel's show window, condoms with beaks, spurs, and comb, with bells; thimbles. The movie house consumptive changes the billboard: today a moonlit bridge beneath pine trees, a face in black and yellow stripes like an Indian fish.)

Gliding in outer space as he was, the Director couldn't take it any longer and, bathed in a sulphurous froth, fell to the floor. María Eng brought in a pillbox of violet salts and a pitcher of orange juice with ice.

The Pekinese flute band had begun the Poem of the Barge's vocal theme, and since once she started Lotus couldn't stop till the grand finale, Help and Mercy popped out of the wings, half-naked, turning somersaults in the air, hummingbirds: they hung their heads back and for a helm used their tails. Sorrel manes, woolen yarn, flame, ribbon of resin, needles, dark green coins, these were the tresses that lamps filtered among curtains imitating curtains of Venetian felt, cardboard walls, bridges, Etruscan birds.

The Divine Ones flew, yes, flew orange-striped, chlorophyll-striped over the stage, suspended by plastic wires the color of the background curtain, the color of the screens in Polynesian brothels and the color of the air a snowy fan displaces.

High up the Smilers howled like castrated rabbits, prayed the salute to the Great Madman and pissed out of fear. They looked down at us; little anteater eyes.

Lotus, in a dragon-drawn cart, struggled with a bigheaded demon and, singing the Kidnap Aria, crossed northern auroras of stage time. Her face was a flat circle, three stripes under a crown of two facing unicorns.

Over the Cantonese band—two blacks and a Cantonese blowing flageolets—the Empress bends backward in the cart, a bamboo shoot pulled by the river's current.

The Director opened a crack in one eye. He said he had been dreaming of Lotus and that she had been a black kite on gold letters and also a bird pierced by a lance and a great key wrapped in feathers.

His head wrapped in vinegar cloths, feet in hot water, two strawberry ices (for the lack of ice) beneath the two little pockets between his legs which, from the fright, had emptied out on him or were at his bellybutton or God knows where:

"The show must go on!"

The Spaniard knocked on the zinc door so hard that the orchestra stopped playing and the stagehand let go of the plastic wires. (The smell of burnt tea, which experienced noses can detect a mile away, attracts the fuzz.) He let go of the plastic wires, as I was saying, and the Fannies fell to the floor demolishing the flushed parts for which they are so named.

So that, on the stage, all three stared at each other. *Faceba proprio pietá.*

The Peeping Tom's walk, and much more so for being a Spaniard's, does not need captions.

If I were you, Lotus dear, I would have realized by now that it's He who's coming, and instead of sitting there, in your steam bath, weighing yourself, drinking vinegar and washing your eyes with salt, I would have bolted my dressing room door by now. In your present state you'll stay chaste and pure as long as it takes to shake a lamb's tail.

Help and Mercy (*playing canasta in the corridor, already dressed for the Amazon number*):

"Good grief! That's all we needed: God the writer, who sees all and knows all before anybody else does, who gives advice and puts his nose in everybody's business but his own!"

Well, as I was saying before the So Full of Graces interrupted me, Peeping Tom, all the time walking diagonally, appears in slice form. Archimboldesque, he's made of parsley, wood, edible snail when he explores the forest; here in the theater corridor where he advances along the wall, he continues sideways: he cuts like a penknife through shit-stained posters, javelins, lutes with little clusters of hashish hidden inside, Persian pillboxes filled with stones and black butterflies.

He moved so angular and diagonally that Lotus didn't see him when, *comme d'habitude,* she came off the stage leaving the audience in standing ovation, fainting spells, and a rainfall of gardenias.

The *regina pictrix* will now go through the twelve stages of self-absorption. She will unmask herself. She will cease to be Empress Ming; she will be a piece of paint-smeared hide.

When the General, with a bunch of roses in one hand and an extra-fine cigar in the other, threw open the door to the Empress's dressing room, he let out a skinny bald Chinaman, in a linen guayabera and slacks, carrying a grapefruit on a tray.

The Battle Lover went inside without so much as a peep. The Chinaman slipped out.

Like a squirrel, the Spaniard looked here and there, sniffing, poking around, looking for his little Chinese cherry, his lychee. He saw a lace slip hanging from a screen and his mouth watered. He tiptoed near. In one stroke he pulled it down. But he didn't hear a scream on the other side. Nor when he went into the bathroom. He also checked behind the doors and under the bed. Where three calico cats stood on one paw, like pelicans or sea horses.

He lost his patience. It was in the closet where he found a black fitted waistcoat and see-through underpants, advertised on television. Like all generals in a tight spot, this one's digestion stopped short on him (lobster Thermidor, one of the fleet's favorite dishes), became a knot in his throat and another in his belly and he could just about utter the all too familiar "Help me, dear God." He walked out, reread the sign on the door. The Empress. He was just about to leave when he heard the racket. The very irritated Symmetrical Ones were coming, their vocabulary in high voltage, counting the evening's earnings between praises, as follows:

"Your mother doesn't know who your father is."

"Daughter of a thousands jisms and all of them different."

"Monkey vulture crossbreed."

They see Medals Galore and break into a strut, here a hip, there a hip, they dance the Scorpion carnival dance, scarcely touching the floor, as when on the blue rug of the first act they bounce among streamers that inscribe the sign of war, keepers that they are of the Secret of the Bounce.

A Sivaic Band

Aren't they cute? Wrapped in fringed mantillas, hair twisted in Borrominesque helices, falling in sea shells, followed by gold threads like the cars of certain nocturnal photographs. That mallow, that lemon tea lotion, that big wicker basket filled with pocketbooks, pineapples, and *caimitos*; that frozen daquiri with strawberries they're drinking, they do everything so *mignonnes!* Isn't that right, General? You could eat them up! How tasty, how crispy! Go ahead, have a bite, mate! They crunch deliciously, like little partridge bones. Come on, General, say something to them, paint the town red, remember the old days at the Louvre Sidewalk Café, not to mention the Marte and Belona dance school soirees.

THE GEN: No sirree, I won't say a thing to them.

I: Come on, don't put us on, such a gentleman as yourself.

THE GEN: And why don't you say something to them? To me they're two ugly ducklings, two Peruvian monkeys.

I: Never mind the rhetoric. Throw them something, even if it's only a pebble, a sigh.

The General bent down with the maximum flexion his venerable somatic vehicle allowed. Seen from the rear guard he was like a tricycle or a photographer with his head inside a box camera. From the prow, an adipose grotto: the three layers of his chin, the ovoid of the Thermidophagus veiled in sparkles, upside-down dome. I don't know how you could see from below because I couldn't bend lower than him, but I imagine that a good background for him would be the theater awning, which is decorated with laurel branches in decalcomania, with suns and stars made of silver paper that flies have profaned.

Given the abundance of arachnids, Coleoptera and other neighbors in the place, the General made sure several times that what he was going to throw them was a pebble and not a centipede, spider, or wasp.

The Tiny Feet were already walking backward when in their ringlets they received the homage.

In the twinkling of an eye the cry "Metamorphosis" was heard in G flat, and the Two immediately appear mounted on racing Vespas, at full speed, and armed with Thompson machine guns, two-tongued knives, javelins, flame-throwers, pum-pum guns, hand grenades and tear-gas bombs. Helmets crown even their helices, all of which is very natural in such a bad neighborhood. What is even more surprising is that each One is supplied with three heads and seven arms. The tetradecapodous and hexacephalous aluminum artifact is a sight to see!

My dear, what a getup! What a Sivaic band! The four femur piccolos tremble under the step of fourteen cornets spitting yellow light, and these under the heads of Tarot Papesses. The albino stream flows through diamonds and clubs.

Help pulls a hair out of this stream, knots it twice and blows upon it, and at the sound of "Metamorphosis!" it turns into a snake that wriggles in the air like a butterfly in someone's mouth, breaks against the ground and becomes a chameleon, toad, giant shrimps. So she populates the square with animals: monkey actors, red antelopes on sun clocks, frightened cranes, camels laden with hydraulic organs, leopards, lynx, bears fleeing from the motor scooters.

Mercy is having a good time, and laughs with a slight hiccup, as if a feather were tickling her bellybutton, until Help starts commanding again and all the creatures, before reaching the sidewalks, are turned into birds and fly away.

The light of the moon comes out as if filtered through an aquarium.

Joined by a bellybutton, Siamese motorcycles, the Vespas duplicate themselves: four opaque triangles. Behind them, a river of metal nuts and rusting tin cans divide an orange and black landscape; they follow its meanderings down empty terraces, aisles of mildewed brass, ashen porticos whose furniture has been bleached by moss.

The Bald Divinities roll along and the squeaking of their tires on the pavement is like that of an orchestra of deaf men, like that of an arm breaking, or a head between cogs. They're moving at top speed. But, do you by any chance think they wobble or wave good-bye? Nothing of the sort: majestic, they wear red scarves, motionless like hanged men's tongues; the air barely grazes their hair…Now they throb, contract, swell, and collapse like salty toads, a Maryan doll that nods, that lets go of its rabbi's bonnet, that asks for water in sign language, that unwinds and has hands that trace a dotted line as they move. That stops.

As the heads of saints on a Yoruba altar shine upon the chalice, surrounded by rotten fruit and beheaded roosters, so among horns and crowbars do the heads of the Living-Dead emerge from a luminous plate: white eyes on white faces, peppermint hair crowned by a halo of flames, two thin threads rolling down from broken eyelids and splitting their faces into stripes, Byzantine coins.

They are fluorescent, they are acetylene, they are drums that hypnotize birds, they are helicopters, they are chairs at the bottom of an aquarium, they are obese eunuchs, their tiny sexes among pink flowers, they are piranhas, leprous angels who sing "Metamorphosis, metamorphosis," they are two unhappy creatures who just wanted to escape a retired Priapus. They are forgiven.

What a change, my frog babies! At the green of the traffic light the Divine Ones reappear in normal state. On their Vespas, dressed in leather, they take off noisily, discharging black smoke through their escape pipes. Mounted on those motor scooters and disguised as juvenile delinquents you girls are as sad as the toy horses on a small town merry-go-round!

The Vespa maneuvers explain many things: Lotus, in a guayabera and a Tyrolean hat that hides her bald pate, has already been doing the rounds for quite a while in her zone on Zanja Street, wearing down heels and sidewalk. With night she falls from dollar to peso, bed to cot, whiskey to coffee, and from yes to *sí*. G. sees her go by and stands there as if he were watching it rain. And she, sadistic, smiles at him.

Nevertheless, G. goes wet all over when he sees the Peripathetics coming. Dressed in black leather from head to toe, they adorn the aforementioned helmets with color pictures of Elvis Presley, James Dean pins, autographs by Paul Anka, locks of hair from Tab Hunter, Pat Boone's fingerprints, and Rock Hudson's *"measurements."*

How great they look! Standing on a corner in open offer and demand in front of a Gravi toothpaste poster (Gravi: "the queen of toothpastes") between the giant toothbrush and the pink spiral.

The General comes over. With such publicity, how can he resist?

HELP (*who, in her black leather jacket, is sweating—average temperature on the "isle" 81 degrees Fahrenheit*): Pretty hot out, huh?

GENERAL: Looks like it's going to rain.

(*Giggles from all sides.*)

As she would a kingdom of heavens according to its snow-falls and birds, so has Dragon Puss divided the sidewalk into beats. She strolls around the bars and pool rooms in a black bonnet, a belt of rhinoceros hide and a marble tablet in her hands. Sententious, she christens herself The Very Old Man. He indicates with a chalk mark the boundaries of the neighborhood—a Gravi poster, the movie billboard, the shadow of the Chinese laundry's neon sign, he names them according to kind, and then goes around on his bicycle, holding out a little box for taxes. He's a pimp by birth; he's a member of the fuzz. He knows where all the grass and all the numbers are and what they're called. He pushes but neither plays nor smokes. He avoids chance and fire. To control the Illusory is to renounce it—he utters, and so, the master-of-every-possible-science does his rounds selling tickets, joints, and even little envelopes of "sugar" (to support native industry—he says). He psalmodiously grants Nirvanas.

The initiate call him Heaven of One Hundred Rainbows, Mount of Flowers and Fruits, Face. He enters the smoking rooms singing and leaves in the pipes and samovars an orange cornea like that of the toucan's beak. Donor of Pools of Jade, he disappears; a resinous smell in the air.

G. goes to all those stops, passes through all those concentric curtains, sinks into all those spirals of smoke inquiring after the sense of his being. He searches for Lotus, searches for Lotus, and pays for his "joints" among mocking giggles.

In those sheds of creaking bamboo they drink the most aged wines to his health; they offer him, so that he may have a taste of "hop," the smoking tubes branching from their pipes. He refuses.

"All my alcohols I carry within me."

He has just consummated with the Two—and both together—the bluff that you are imagining. Of course, said fate was perpetuated sadistically and even in his moments of greatest suffocation (which he suffered, dressed as he was in coat and underpants), G. did not halt his interrogation:

G. (*his tins clanking along with his seesawing*): Where is the Empress, my honey-pie, my little moon-shaped fanny?

And the PERIPATHETICS (*in duet*): The Empress is a mirage, a *trompe-l'œil,* a flower *in vitro.*

And G. (*whipping their waxy behinds*): Ming exists. I've seen her in the forest (*and a lash*), I've seen her on stage (*and another*).

> Where have you hidden away
> leaving me in such dismay?

And the PAINTED LADIES: Ming is pure absence, she is what she is not. There is no water for your thirst.

Etc., etc.

What an inquisition, my Frog Babies! You must have charged the Spaniard twenty dollars service *non compris* plus hotel and dinner—that steamed cinnamon milk you so much adore—.

EYEBROWS GALORE: Ah yes, some inquisition that was. With the heat and his combinatory mania. He wore himself out in all the Possibles.

I: Well it doesn't seem so. Look. He's heading for Eng zone.

EYES GALORE (*waving big pearl and tortoise-shell fans*): Fine, but what's he going to practice?—and with what?—(*horselaughs*). He's just realized that as we share our zone, since when one wears out her charms contending among feathers, the other refreshes them with new recruits from the show windows, María also shares hers, with Lotus Flower. In María he may find the mediation, the being.

He's now on the other side of the Gravi sign. Sweltering, but in high spirits. He's in Eng zone. From her first round of the night María has left a fragrance of jasmine and water lily; in the dew on the pavement her steps are written, on the show windows the soft brush of her gauze, in the air the mahogany wake of her pearl-braided bun.

Dragon Puss walks by. Behind her, María. G. comes alongside and woos her. He invites her to a daiquiri at the Two Worlds Bar, to another, and then confesses that he's an initiate in the numbers, in the permutations. Thus his fascination for the "theater," and mirrors. He yearns for the double, the symmetrical, the Cartesian devil who comes from the other side of the stage to give himself his reply—you and I—which turns inside out like a glove.

She gets the picture, but says neither yes nor no. She

veils her face with her bamboo necklaces. Behind them she smiles. The quiver of the beads is like that of jet black adding beads. Her eyes are like two piggy bank holes, two mechanical lanterns. Now she puts them on high beam; a sailor is approaching.

She leaves with him. She tells G. to wait, "after all, mister is only interested in me anyway," tomorrow is another day.

G. jumped without impulse. Toy soldier. Where was that wind coming from? His stool was whirling. He was out on the street when he felt someone grab him by the arm. It was the waiter. He hadn't paid.

He watches her crumble among letters. Magnified red numbers. Strips of white fabric that are walls. Now she's a Melanesian lute. A bird from the Asiatic tropics on the other side of a river. Of rose ashes.

(*Drum roll*)

It's his footsteps. Military, what else. Does he hear the bagpipes of a march? Does he receive voices of command? María is slipping away from him—snake in water—; and him, after her of course. At full speed. Off he goes. Greyhound after a tin partridge, tiger after a wild pigeon stuck to his own self. His femurs creak. Bloodhound. Tongue hanging out. Wet buck. Strip of scattered hoops. Leaves black lines. Greyhound dog, Shell dragon.

She, there, faraway. He calls to her, puts her together like a puzzle, draws her by joining numbers. Sniffs her— rum, cinnamon, brown sugar—; yes, sniffs her: the Peeping Tom is myopic.

As in a theater when the actor exclaims: "Oh, here is

the dawn!" and all the gold spots go on in unison, so, all of a sudden, does the Havana night fall. G., lost. María is that dampness, that absence of birds, the gong at the Opera, its racket—reverberation of tambourines, mildewed cymbals—and the successive shadows it leaves in the air; snakes battling among glass, rotting orchids, typhoon, anis stones growing in bottles, war of Burmese jaguars.

Aporia of Action, María is Desire, the Absence of Lotus. G.: a little blind man being bluffed. He feels around in the void, he's going to touch her, yes, he jumps on her, grabs her.

"Hey, what's up fella? Can't a girl have some peace in this city?"

He had caught the singer at the Picasso Club, who was just leaving the floor.

He sees her again. There she goes. This time it was her. She disappears into the stores, among paper lanterns. A sweet smell of *lukum*. G. zigzags. Follows himself. Propelled photograph, almost whole, it moves, paler, behind his own body, and again, blurred, behind him…and again. It's an army. They look at each other in a mirror and step back: dark green, olive faces, grapefruit, dry grass; pyramidal beards of astrakhan, black wool, brown fibered curls; gray cork stains, algae. They see themselves sewn with medals and tricolored bands, ribbons and braids; they see themselves outlined on damasks, on Toledan lace; they see themselves mended with pieces of curtains, gold bees and fleurs-de-lis, tapestries of roses and Flemish apples and serpents. Yes, they take a step backward: with good reason. The honor of the navy!

>Lola, lola
>la la la la
>Ich bin die fesche Lola

"What happened?"

Well, pursuing María and the American, bouncing from screen to screen, G. has ended up inside this *café-concert*. He flops down into a wicker chair—Cantonese girls bring him palm leaves and slippers—and asks for a "cuba-libre." He finally has them: there they are, rubbing each other to music, next to the Charleston band pianola. María, beneath blue oil lamps, her open hands on the *boy's* shoulder, winks at a green-eyed mulatto marimba player. Johnny Smith draws her closer. He's very smiley, red-headed and freckled, wears white sailcloth pants that pinch his little ass and a fluorescent poppy shirt which is why G. can see him despite night and myopia.

The girls who are singing and wiggling and riding painted wood pelicans and cloth bats on the platform in the back are the Baby Faces. My, those girls have changed! You've got to admit, the Secret of the Transformations does outrageous things! Now they're fat ladies with rubbery bellies crowned in hats made of pheasants in a plate of golden fruit, feather boats, merlons. They're the bearded ladies of a Mongol circus. Their four parallel feet tap against the stage boards and raise a yellow dust. They shout: "Lola, Lola." Then Chong and Si-Yuen appear through the side doors—the Tallow Ones do not wish to renounce their former apparitions, so beautiful do they find them, and their show goes on at the Opera—dressed in pieces of red and gold fabric, blond like dolls, burning from alcohol, their blue blue eyes enveloped in black stripes, Klimt's sad muses. They dance a two-step, wrapped in the same garland. Fascinated by that dancing symmetry, G. doesn't see the Roly-Polies open up, let Eng and Johnny through and close again, joining at the middle line, like the shutters of a triptych.

(*Black out*)

HEL. and MER.: No! We are the Light. We've simply become her absence. Now we're her islands. Look!

Yes, the ceiling, the floor and the walls are red, blue, and yellow disks that revolve at full speed and cut into each other and light up and go out and are of another red and another violet and explode and cut into each other again. Until the General rubs his eyes.

He flings himself against a wall and goes through it.

He is on the other side.

It is a dark private room, smelling of mentholated Camel smoke. Four black leather sofas in the corners. Mirrors. On a wall lit by a small white lamp, a man is painting. Opposite him—G. sees them reflected—María and *il rosso* are kissing; they sit side by side and look at the wall (where the fresco is gradually taking shape). They caress each other and smile. He shows her his sex, pink and perfectly cylindrical, the glans is a snail or a dome striped in white and the fluorescent poppy of his shirt, like a candy cane or a pinwheel. María touches it with the tips of her fingers. Giggling. Now she shows him her breasts, identically decorated: a yellow spiral starts from each nipple and disappears on her chest; she shows him her navel: painted: the

43

miniature reproduction of a round concave molding. Johnny glues his eye to her stomach to see it. A raging sea takes up almost half the sphere—continuous lines in black ink, like the veins of a tree—where he can vaguely make out a boat. To the right a cliff, foam surrounding the rocks, a sky of red marks.

MARÍA (*very proud*): Pretty, huh?

Johnny agrees with a nod.

MARÍA (*professional*): The original, attributed to Li Sung, who according to our chronology lived between 1166 and 1243, is called "In a boat," and is the leaf of a fan-shaped album, sketched in ink and dye on silk.

JOHNNY: How I would like to have one!

MARÍA (*pointing to the painter*): He's the one who makes them, Little Torture Face, very ancient master in the symmetrical arts of pleasure and horror to the eyes: Chinese Painting and Torture.

G.: Hey, what's up?

It's the Mistresses-of-All-Appearance who are taking revenge on G. (cf. blows and lashes during that foolish act, remember?) and they reveal themselves as fluorescent Light. Yes, a great circular neon lamp lights up the room. The turtledoves leap up and dress. G. is exposed in all his deceit: the Peeping Tom was in his Nirvana and, from mere contemplation, had already passed to *praxis da solo.* He was forgetting about Lotus. Or had he substituted the duo with her (and himself as the mister) ?

Little Torture Face is now standing (he really does have a scary face: swords for eyebrows; green and orange stripes run across his forehead and circle his eyes, black ones cross his cheeks and nose and turn into flowers; and a tiger mouth).

Now in front of G. he scolds him, waving his paint-stained hands in his face.

"You Peeping Tom, you heel, what the hell are you doing here?"

G. backs up.

And Little Face—"Give me that hand."

He grabs G.'s right hand.

"Here, that'll teach you."

And he tears off a nail.

He knocked on the walls and ceiling. He left a fresh labyrinth on the floor: the thread of blood from his pinky. Cold sweat. A ringing in his ears, a fistful of fig salt on his tongue; rubber legs, vinegar eyes. His night was pierced by green lights like those of the Feast of the Lanterns. Yes, what General can stand the sight of blood? He wouldn't look at his hand, the wet pinky.

He threw himself against a door. An old lady opened it, her face painted white, her lips very red. She kowtowed, and bandaged his hand in a cold compress.

"We were waiting for you," she said, and she brought him a cup of dragon eye soup. G. tried it, and had a whiff of cinnamon syrup along with soaking lye, hot irons, old clothes, and grease.

"I suffer in a laundry"—added the Venerable One—"but believe it or not, I was born with a black jade stone in my mouth, I slept in beds of sandalwood and was an imperial concubine. I strive among soaking underwear but I have drunk the tea of the thousand red drops and the pollen wine of a hundred roses, sap from a thousand trees, unicorn marrow and phoenix milk. Like you, I am expiating here. Come through this corridor. Be careful. Don't dirty the sheets."

G. followed close behind the Chinese woman. ("I have fever.") And covering his nose (they were passing between tubs of rotting lye where pieces of blue soap and towels were floating).—"What a plebeian stench!"

"Wait here for me."

It was a room with a counter full of ironed shirts and bags of borax. A calendar hung from a shelf, the picture was a Chinese girl (her face flat, as if they were pressing it against a window) in a bikini, riding a Vespa; a portable refrigerator, a portable radio, a movie camera and a family-sized Coca Cola in an ice bucket bursting from its bags. Written between black marks, down by the wheels, was MODERN CHINA. G. was going to look at the next illustration when a hatch door opened in the floor and the old woman's head came out.

"Come down this way."

The small slimy staircase led him to another dark room. Dampness stained the walls. The Venerable One disappeared. Little Torture Face entered. He wore a purple cap, two gold dragons chasing the same pearl girded his forehead. Dressed in mauve, a flowered scarf of Japanese satin. Entwined in the scarf, a braid of pearls bearing the eight emblems of the Taoist saints, disappearing behind a belt of tassels.

"Don't try to fool me, General old boy"—and he gave him a quick, violent tap on the shoulder which plopped him on his ass. (Although he looked like a painted goose, Little Face was a black belt in the ring.)

"That's right, don't try to fool me: I know all about it. Don't lose your time answering back. I know alchemy, the sublimation of the vital elixir, the concoction and reduction of cinnabar. How could I not be wise to your tricks? Listen carefully. Just listen carefully: either you stop chasing Lotus Flower or I eliminate you. Get it? I eliminate you. Want me to bury you in ice? Stick burning matches into the soles of your feet? Want me to cut them off with a Gillette blue blade? No? Then take it easy. Lotus and María. Leave them alone. Okay, Gen?"

The floor was made of boards and smelled of cat urine. He remembered that the old woman had given him a cup of tea and that while drinking he had fallen asleep. Had many days passed? Was it all a dream? Was he still dreaming?

It was day. What surprised him most was not waking up on the floor, in a stinking pigsty, but rather finding out, in the light which shone through a crack, that what he thought were damp spots was a fresco which decorated all four walls and the wooden door. In it appeared Little Torture Face, the two Fat Ladies, Chong and Si-Yuen, all with shaven skulls, naked to the navel and barefoot, on top of clouds whose edges were like the waves of the round molding. Miss Chong, in profile, wearing a red cape and gold earrings and gazing into space, was pointing to a long-bristled brush, or a fly swat. Little Face was untying a parchment and receiving an artist's brush from Si-Yuen. One Fat Lady held up a red receptacle and a staff with four gargoyles, the other, with her little white feet in

47

the foam, opened her left hand in a U, as if she were out-lining a flower, and separated the small pointy and spread-ing fingers of her right, letting go of coins—or bread crumbs.

Behind the cloud a cliff. Black and fluffy trees, with sharp leaves. A waterfall.

G. peeped into the waters—the crack in the door—. And discovered:

a. that he was in a cellar,

b. that the cellar was the laundry,

c. that in the adjoining room there was a silent meeting of smokers.

Orange smoke. Among tea kettles and blue cups he made out María's head, and those of the little Ophidia Eyes, back in their forms as chorus girls of the Opera (what hap-pened to the Fat Ladies?), covered with stuffed humming-birds, *guacamayos* and candied pineapples with rubies; also Dragon Puss, the Director, and another Chinaman, thin and wiry like an eel, bald, and mustard yellow. He was in the center of the chorus, standing and naked (yes, he had one, but small and spiraled like a little screw) next to Little Torture Face, in underpants.

The *Biondas* served tea, and politely handed around sugar cubes and small pieces of grapefruit, or *lukum,* or something coated with flour.

Mustard scratched his bald pate, made three bows, and in a faint whistle voice, like a goosed monkey's, he hummed:

"The being of the birds is not the tone of the trills but feathers falling at each change. White, they are other birds in the snow, the signature of the first; red, fish that becomes butterfly when attacked. Another when it changes, goes off course leaving small snake eyes among its old feathers: endows its fraud with a gaze; its joy is to stick itself in the air in front of its blind double, to place the tigers face to face with the Apocrypha."

> Oh, ardent!
> Oh, ferocious!
> Oh, sweet birds!

But G. was not able to listen to more. Opening the body of one of the Fat Ladies in the fresco along the middle line (the navel was the lock on the door), the ex-mandarin woman entered the cellar.

"La Hang medicine! Believe it or not, I know the Books by heart. The gentleman is cured." (*And she pulls off the bandage.*) G. withdraws his hand, like the claw of a boiled crab.

He's out on the street.

Already the screens are opening, the Venetian blinds falling with a sound of sand, the milkmen on their rounds.

The matron from Formosa washes her face. And opens a can of sardines.

G. no longer eats or sleeps. He gets cramps, visions, constipation. He feels looked at (but no grass, no, just coffee, which he takes to perk up, and tranquilizers, which he takes to calm down), he weathers storms in a wine cup— tea he no longer takes—he's all choked up, something's pressing his throat. Are they hanging a rag doll in his image somewhere? Are they sticking pins in the eyes of his

49

photograph behind some door? Is his name in a glass of vinegar? He doesn't know. At night he searches. Absence eats his liver—ontological cirrhosis—. After all it's the poor Mrs. General who pays for the broken plates. With all this nonsense it turns out that Medals Galore no longer rends her homage. She cries behind screens, takes refuge in the cellar with her supply of snuff…but no luck. Neither oysters nor Ovaltine in condensed milk: there isn't an aphrodisiac that works. G. remains in the doorhead (or on the threshold, which in this case is the same thing); it gives him claustrophobia.

THE GENERAL: For the Virgin of Covadonga, this is overdoing it! You lie: I've never neglected my conjugal duties. I deliver efficiently and attentively twice a week, Mondays and Thursdays, to be exact.

I: That's what he says. The truth is that Mrs. General…

THE (*more and more hypothetical*) READER of these pages: Okay, make up your minds: one version or the other. What I want is facts. Yes, facts, action, development, message, in short. Lyrical message!

As I was saying: For G. the Theater became Mass. Always in the first row. The appearance of Lotus in the Capture of the Fort is the celebration of all the Possibles. In the deceptive, in the ontic, he takes shadow for substance. During intermission he knocks his head against Nothingness. He goes to the dressing rooms and, in keeping with the ancient feudal custom, drops a jade bracelet outside the Empress's door to gain her favors. Always freshly starched, always with his Romeo and Juliet and his jacket, which already displays concentric strata of different blues in its armpits—sweat permits the dating of it like the cortex of trees—and that faint smell of sweet wine with egg yolk, his morning restorative.

He knows the Capture by heart: he yawns during the decagonal ambush, during the dance of the knives and even during the clash between Meng Hai-Kung and the government troops. He weeps when Lotus appears between two *sheng* players, a javelin in each hand, dressed in blue leaves, crowned with two pheasant feathers. In her face fishes sail, black butterflies flee over her eyelids. Two white spirals divide her forehead; two geometrical fringes, black and yellow, start from her upper lip and sailing around her nose, open like spirals on her cheeks. Two masks resembling her face are painted on her sleeves. A gold cord hangs from the hilt of the sword she wears on her belt. Lotus is here. LOTUS EXITS. Lighter than the sound of the choral *b,* more delicious than ruby wine and cocoanut milk.

Two color sergeants follow her with the blue Flag of the Empire, which bears a letter in its center; behind them the band players: two pipe, two lute, and a *tan-pin-ku.*

Phoenix of the mountain, the Moon illumines her. The Moon is an oscillating lantern; her eyes black darts.

Even after the banquet ginger can celebrate with its seven flavors, and after the rain light with its seven islands: when the acrobats leave Lotus surrenders her best high kung notes. She stands on tiptoe, fills herself with air and emits them effortlessly, perforating hearts and eardrums. She advances with the clashing of cymbals and drum rolls; she steps back and the Queen of Cranes (do you recognize her? can you guess who it is? Take a good look and you'll know—answer two lines below) and the Queen of

Falcons (who in the legend is a King, but even metamorphosis has its limits) appear. That's right, you've guessed it, *Chong* and *Si-Yuen,* the Neat Ones, the Mistresses-of-the-Grass-of-Immortality, do battle before Lotus, jump over one another, spin cartwheels, rush on with serrated machetes and bows. Thus they lose their feathers on stage. Behind, Lotus, the Fixed One, smiles, absent, holding in her hand the imperial Phoenix, flanked by two unicorns. There she is, in full possession of her Yin, as you saw her in the forest, remember?

G. (*tearful, il povero*): Yes, of course I remember, by the ferns, near the Almendares…

I: Quiet. Listen to her. She's singing her solo.

G. (*sighing*): How lovely this all is!

I (*who wakes him up*): Come down from that cloud and return to reality. The Capture of the Fort is over.

(*applause, etc.*)

At Home with the General

G. (*angry, purple veinlets furrow his triple chin*): All I want to know is where she is, who she is, why she doesn't come, where does she hide herself, where.

And he shakes them by the shoulder. Feathers, lice, and spangles come off. Now they're baldpates.

THEY (*the only girls who, shook up, become two baldpates*): We can't just say it any old way. She's a secret, she's an appearance, she's…

The insipid things guffaw, crack up, hop around, they're leap frogs, they're about to come apart.

GENERAL (*confidentially*): I just want you to tell her it's me, the one from the Forest, tell her I go to the theater every day and that (and his eyes water—are you going to cry? come on, men don't cry—it's really pitiable) I can't go on like this.

THE JERKS: We'll tell her.

And so, the big sports put everything in the basket that strikes their fancy, taking advantage of G.'s moment of weakness.

For my room! (*it's Help*). And she grabs an engraving, an ivory fan. Now, graceful, she fans herself like a Spanish girl at a country fair, moving her eyes to the beat, striking her heels against the floor. Olé!

The Other, more discreet, but more jeeringly plays with the angora cats, who run around dragging along ribbons and bells and get caught on the legs of rocking chairs. She prefers the small sphinx heads, hourglasses, stuffed storks, the little jade Chinamen who serve as lamp supports, the big fat angels in gilded wood. She's a Pop initiate, she's quite *à la page*. She's singing, and putting all she can get her hands on into a crate.

G. (*endearingly*): Take everything you want. Tell her to be so good as to look at me.

Oh, this is too much. Look at that. Help is dragging a red marble bathtub mounted on four bronze paws toward the street. What she'll do with it I don't know, because when it comes to taking a bath, only once in a blue moon and even then you have to make her.

Help (*there is no insult worse than the truth*): And you, mind your own business, shithead, this I got for you.

And the smutty creature shows me an enormous porphyry phallus, almost a yard long, that she's taking for her "Pompeian Room." You should see her, she's in it up to her neck. Her Vespa is overloaded and now she's calling for a pickup truck.

The Other, more satiable, is hanging around, chatting with Mrs. General, spinning cartwheels on a Persian rug (which she'll surely take with her) with an albino girl squeezed into a tight red dressing gown—could she be G.'s granddaughter?—. Hurrah! They look like two gladiators.

They sped away, thundering, on their motor scooters. Crossing their fingers they go. They didn't miss a single brooch. They ride in kimonos, and silk hats. They even carry lighted lamps in blue ceramic—battery-run—on their handlebars. Their bags are full of Bibles, paperweights, clocks, etc. The Insatiables didn't leave a thing.

G.: Not a thing! Regard the tables: dust. But not all is lost.

Better said:

When G. saw that all was lost and already in *articulo mortis,* he thought up a final appeal. He gave the Nymphs, on condition that they hand it to her as she came off the stage, a present for Lotus. A smitten heart stops at nothing!

"What was it?"

Well outwardly, nothing special. Just another bracelet, the usual fare, in blue jade, with painted flowers and butterflies, like those the Mongolian peasant women wore. Of course this one had, besides, an inner device that would work upon closing the jewel on the wrist: it would spring out two very sharp little razor blades against the inner part of the fist. Yes, just what you're thinking, slit arteries. It's true: G. had ended his parable, completed his parabolic cycle. From Peeping Tom to sadist. He who possesses with the eye possesses with the dagger. He would recognize her by her blood. Wound her. Pleasure is crossed with pain.

Does he feel guilty? Hardly. Like they say, the Spaniard bit went to his head. He's a vampire.

But, a last question remains:

"Where do all those objects come from, where has the preceding scene unfolded?"

Well, so intense was the pilgrimage of his nights and the impatience of his days, that G. decided to change tactics. What was needed in the Theater? What did Lotus use every day? What could she not live without?

Although his calling was great, he soon rejected the idea of a grocery store. In Lotus's kitchen, according to the laws of the Opera, almost everything was excluded. The rice with tea that she'd eat and the sesame seed oil that she'd massage herself with did not justify setting up shop. He decided on what was left. So, with his last savings, Mrs. General, the cats, and the albino jumper whom you have just seen, along with some war and hunting trophies, G. settled in Chinatown *de plein pied*. There, across the street from the theater, he opened *Divine Providence,* super store, the one the Magpies recently ravaged.

There he stands guard day and night. Sentinel in his stockade.

Today he's not going to the show.

He's waiting for them to carry a pale body out the stage door.

DOLORES RONDON _____

Since it's such a hot day, it won't do us any harm to take a
walk in the cemetery: marble is cooling, almost like lemonade. There are no café tables or one-armed bandits in
this garden of stone, but we'll come to that. In this part of
Camagüey, in the center of Cuba, there's no end of oil
portraits, of dead black men looking rosier and healthier
than they ever did alive, or of two-story chapels, or reading material. Here at this crossroads, for example, you
can read Dolores Rondón's poem:

> Dolores Rondón did here
> reach the end of her career,
> come mortal, and ponder
> on where lies true grandeur.
> Pride and arrogance,
> power and prominence,
> all is bound to perish.
> And you only immortalize
> the evil you economize
> and the good you may cherish.

A Hard Profession, Dolores's. Courtesan and poet. Courtesan all her life. Poet for a day. But time dissolves it all, like the sea into the sea. Of the courtesan, and her ups and downs, which were those of the senator Mortal Pérez, nothing remains. But the poet views us, from death.

Under the poem two angels face down hold up a lighted lamp.

A lighted lamp over a ribbon inscribed in Latin.

A ribbon inscribed in Latin tied around a bunch of flowers.

And all in marble!

But let's give our two narrators the floor. Let them present the life of Dolores Rondón. They won't do it in chronological order, but in that of the poem, which, after all, is the true one.

Dolores Rondon Did Here

In the provinces, the recent republican era

NARRATOR ONE (*chorus leader with a squeaky, biting voice*):
Ah yes, going back to writing again, what an emetic! As if all this had some purpose, as if all this would penetrate some thick skull, occupy some driveling reader curled up in his armchair before the soporific stew of everyday living!

NARRATOR TWO (*high-sounding, solemn chorus leader, with a deep-chested voice*): That's it, decipher it or bust: all has a purpose, all is final, all returns to all, that is, to nothing, nothing is all (*his throat rasps*)...with this play on words I mean that your emetic is very useful, useful because emetic, in short, with words you modify things, behaviors, the behavior of the (*he stops short, stamps his cothurnus on the floor*).

NARRATOR ONE (*very high pitched*): Behavior, future, modify: lame words. Please, it only hurts when I laugh. You have a mangy dog, I say mangy for example, well then, you take the dog, which is the word, and throw a pail of boiling water on him, which is the exact sense of the word. What does the dog do? What does the word do? And so we have dog-word, water-sense: These are the four parts. Take them! Who pins the tail on the donkey? Here is the summary of my metaphor: lame words for lame realities that follow a lame plan drawn up by a lame monkey.

NARRATOR TWO: I'm slow I admit, but I don't get who the monkey is.

NARRATOR ONE (*in coloratura soprano*): My son, please, when will you learn! (*he looks for an easy comparison*) Now then: words are like flies, toads, as you know, eat flies, snakes eat toads, bulls eat snakes and men eat bulls, that is to say...

NARRATOR TWO: Men eat flies!

NARRATOR ONE: It's not that easy, but enough, we didn't meet here today for that, but to discuss, under the denomination of the Patron Saint of Small Animals, to discuss I say, the case of the mulatto Dolores Rondón.

NARRATOR TWO (*answering a riddle*): The one who reached the end of her career?

NARRATOR ONE: They're one and the same. Let's talk about her.

CLEMENCY (*red-headed and waxen youth with a high and hysterical voice*): With chapter and verse!

HELP (*red-headed and waxen youth with a high and hysterical voice*): With toad tack!

MERCY (*red-headed and waxen youth with a high and hysterical voice*): With monkey fine stone and cats fly cabala!

NARRATOR ONE (*protesting*): Oh no, out of the question! I will not stand for those three queens, horrible creatures.

NARRATOR TWO: Come on, for God's sake (a figure of speech), more simplicity, more modesty. Throw your spangles into the well and listen quietly. These are Dolores's witnesses, her attendants. Let them express themselves.

HELP (*leading a protest by the trio, real leader of the masses style, very confident*): We strive to come out!

MERCY (*sprecht-gesang*): Like the tortoise from his shell,
     like the chicken from his egg,
     like the corpse from his hole, yes!

NARRATOR ONE (*frightened before the apparition of the three acolytes*): Please!

DOLORES (*Wifredo Lam, mulatto woman, voice between a guitar and an obatala drum*): You've got to get out. (*Without any gradation: a street near the station. Rundown hotels. A smell of tobacco and mangos. In the lemon-colored air the red cap of the porters, the clicking of spurs. Street cries. Jewelry vendors. Perhaps the horn of an old Ford.*) Get out of the hole. If you don't change, you get stuck. You've got to keep moving. No, it's not the mud that bothers me, nor the heavy rains, nor the puddles, nor the oxcarts, nor the electoral campaigns; it's the other people buying and selling, buying machetes, soap, knockers, scissors, earrings, rags, old cots and bottles; the others eating and sleeping.

(*The street disappears just as it had appeared.*)

NARRATOR ONE: Now do you see? She despises the essential, the place of her birth.

NARRATOR TWO: Shut up, stupid. The essential is somewhere between the *guanábana* and the *mango*.

DOLORES (*conscious of the narrators' interruption*): I'm getting out of here and I've come to sell all I've got: a wristwatch and a fine Grade A rooster. I can make it to Camagüey easy on what I get. This is it. I'm doing like Christopher Columbus, who burnt his ships behind him. I'm a high-class dancer, let the others have the box step rumba. Learned, I am, well-read, no. My saints I know by heart, and I play the right numbers. Show and place.

HELP (*quickly*): Hey, what's all this about "play"?

MERCY (*erudite*): Each animal is a number of the lottery, one is the horse, nine the snake.

CLEMENCY (*in false falsetto*): Which eats toads, which eats bulls.

DOLORES: I am the legitimate daughter of Ochum, queen of the river and the sky. You got to move fast. You got to keep moving ahead, like a train. You got to get out of here.

NARRATOR ONE: That's what she thinks, that she's going, but she's staying here, here's where her career ends.

NARRATOR TWO (*grandiloquent*): She's going, she's going so that the poem may come true, so that, as I was saying, fate may exist, and the emetic be useful.

DOLORES (*who has overheard the conversation*): What? What are those two old goats over there saying? That I'm staying? That here's where my career ends? We'll see about that. Hey there, Spaniard baby! Yeah you, with the beret.

MORTAL (*blondie, piñata eyes, the man from Castille, with his pure Castillian diction*): Are you calling me?

HELP (*recitative, the voice of a hoarse soprano, glad to see the poem is following its course*): Opposites attract!

MERCY (*and he powders his nose*): Their vertices touch!

CLEMENCY (*crowned with marble garlands*): Like the snake its tail!

HELP, MERCY, CLEMENCY (*dissonant requiem*): Like the beginning its end! (*The three in* guanábana *hats, holding baskets of sugar cones, jumping over the tracks, the train is coming!*)

Reach the End of Her Career

In the provinces, after the fall of Mortal

NARRATOR TWO: Now look where we are! What did I tell you? Her attendants abandoned her, leaving her to her executioner just as they left her to her lovers before, always to the best bidder.

NARRATOR ONE: It's not their fault, they didn't mean to. They revealed the place where Dolores meets her lovers and that's all. For a few coins, for a few cartons of

Chesterfields and an Elizabeth Arden lotion they've sold her, the frivolous lads. They didn't know what they were risking, they didn't know that death was watching at every step. But let's not name Lady Bones, the Lonely Anima, let us not anticipate her arrival. Trusting, they were, are, victims of the mustached fury. They should be warned: Oyá is dread and comes by every day with her cart, mistress of the ways of the wind, of the keys to the cemetery. Dolores is going to die, perhaps is already dying so that the poem may come true. In the heat, in a bug-ridden bed she is dying, without the air conditioning she lived her better days in, always on Very Cold, without her Simmons mattresses, the best in comfort, without the rose water that once perfumed her. Lady Bones, make her...

HELP (*realizing the evil he has done*): All must perish!

MERCY (*and he sprays himself from head to toe with an atomizer*): We are nothing!

CLEMENCY (*and he combs his hair*): From dust to dust!

DOLORES (*With this monologue Dolores receives death. She no longer fears the grandiloquent tone, ridiculous images, folklore, verbosity itself. Dolores enters death in a major key, as she once entered life. She draws out certain words, the names of saints, in this "lyrical declamation." Tearful comicality. Here the rhetoric, and on the patios in the background, the cha-cha-cha*): The river returns to the source, the light to dawn, the wounded beast to the forest. Each one in his water. Each bird in his air. I return to the bottom of the sea, in the god Obatalá's white dressing gown, in the night, flag of the dead. I am a tree, I threw a shadow. Darkness frightens the birds, but day is coming, roosters' watch. Valley of shadow, come to me! The son of Elegua lacks neither bread, nor pasture, nor the chosen water of repose, nor her husband the fragrant fruit. Guitars, I was wood; let my death warm ye. Maracas, break, untuned goddesses. The saints had said it with their daily signals: the broken glass of water, the frisky horses, the black in the mirrors. I didn't hear. I didn't believe. I didn't open the door. Ye were calling. Let the king of the heavens open to me now with the same smile with which I now open, not to every day's lover, but to the murderer. The gods provide for the Damp House the same as they do for the earth. There will be heat, there will be wine and coffee in death. Neither bread, nor pineapple, nor open mamey, nor beheaded roosters will be wanting in my tomb. Nor the oration of the nine days, nor mourning, nor the abundant banquet with guayaba and cheese. Let there be rum at my wake. Rum and rumination. No weeping, no teeth gnashing, no torn clothing. King, receive me; I go without fear. Wind swallow me. Scatter me in the rain...And ye, dark servants, beasts who have betrayed me, may war decimate ye, lightning blind ye, leprosy corrode ye. Ye have promised without keeping your word, gods of whites. Dagger, be brief. Do not repeat my blood.

(*The cha-cha-cha goes off.*)

HELP: A ridiculous farewell monologue. Lacking in Camagüeyan spontaneity.

MERCY: Let the dead have fame, but the living love!

CLEMENCY: What I wouldn't do for a nice cold beer!
NARRATOR TWO: Dumb Fates. Owl faces.
NARRATOR ONE: It's late. Let's go. There's a Caridad del
    Cobre Fair and tonight everybody's drunk.

(*Dolores screams. The cha-cha-cba begins again.*)

(*In the brothel next door, Help, Mercy, and Clemency dance
it and wave their tresses—slow whirls of flame—patting their
lips, biting their fingers, pulling off their cartilage bone necklaces, breaking off their eyebrows, their faces now quartered,
pale masks.*)

COME, MORTAL, AND PONDER

In the provinces, before the election

NARRATOR ONE (*ironical*): Remember the dog?
NARRATOR TWO (*as lost as a nun in a garage*): What dog?
    The one in the manger?
NARRATOR ONE: No, the other more mongrel one, that
    came shooting out in the first line when they threw a
    bucket of boiling water on him.
NARRATOR TWO: Good Heavens! Of course I remem-
    ber. What's become of him?
NARRATOR ONE: You'll know soon enough. Wait. Look:
    they're already there, they're already arriving.
NARRATOR TWO: Who are those people?
NARRATOR ONE: The nomination people, Mortal's
    people.

NARRATOR TWO: The watch of the living and the dead!
(*Multitudes in the square. Cheers, applause. Pennants. Arches
    of triumph pop up all over the place.*)

MORTAL (*aspiring candidate to the municipal council. The
    voice of the first line has become authoritarian*): I...(*but
    there are defects in the microphone, in the radio. First like
    "static," to such a point that you can hear only one syl-
    lable, then the dial goes through all the stations. Sharp
    whistle.*)

(*Singing commercial*) Candado Soap leaves your clothes
    (*spoken, a feeble voice*) or in the Gentleman of the R
    (*intellectual's voice*) Wallraf-Richartz-Museum (*spoken*)
    and in a situation that is internal ext (*sung, Ella
    Fitzgerald*) in the moon.

MORTAL (*continuing the speech*): I, suh (*but the "static" re-
    turns*).

NARRATOR TWO (*afraid*): Looks like the gods are against
    him. He can't even begin his message.

NARRATOR ONE (*a quick giggle*): Message? For there to
    be a message (*repeating something he doesn't understand,
    and that he's just read somewhere*) there must be: num-
    ber one, intentionality; two, a consciousness of the
    transmitter; three, a code; four.

MORTAL (*continuing his speech*): I, son of this Province, on
    this day have received the nomination as candidate
    to the municipal council of Camagüey, the loveliest
    land that human eyes have ever seen, to occupy a
    position in the government of the Republic (*applause*).
    Others will say that...

NARRATOR ONE (*erudite*): The parts of a speech are

known: introduction, thesis, antithesis, refutation, and summary.

MORTAL: It's easy to promise prosperity before you're in power; for us power will not be a triumph but a sacrifice, just as the Nation is an altar, not a pedestal. We will confront those who waste and stake the national treasury in risky pacts or disturbing and reckless exchanges with planned finance and welfare programs for our peasants which includes the building of cheap housing, roads, schools and medical aid, not to forget school breakfast (*applause*), the creation of dance centers, circuses, cockfights, fairs (*applause*) as you have all requested with unanimous enthusiasm.

NARRATOR ONE (*laughing at* MORTAL *for using the word enthusiasm without knowing its root*): Listen to that!

MORTAL (*after listening to him*): Yes, with unanimous enthusiasm, all you illustrious citizens of this glorious and twice heroic town. The voice of rebellion (*in that moment a dog crosses the square where the meeting's taking place, howling like a condemned soul out of Dante's Hell, among applause and cheers, while* HELP, MERCY, *and* CLEMENCY *scream and lose their feathers.*)

HELP, MERCY, CLEMENCY: Watch out! He has rabies!

NARRATOR ONE (*priestly*): Canis hydrophobus, Dominus Tecum!

HELP, MERCY, CLEMENCY: Amen!

NARRATOR TWO: Aha, those vipers again, those venomous poisons, fresh, newly bathed, bleached salmon and wearing zebra-skin boots, I knew I smelled Camels and Shoulton Old Spice. There they are, after perpetrating the most bloodcurdling crime in Camagüeyan history, the most ignoble betrayal, a fratricide that's so…I cannot find the adjective.

HELP, MERCY, CLEMENCY (*witches' cackles before a concoction of vinegar and salty toads*).

HELP: Poor devil, he doesn't understand a thing. He has no discrimination whatsoever. Look, it's enough to enumerate in one stroke all your errors: they are colossal, dropsical, whale-sized. Look, it's enough to point out four (*sure of himself, an academic reading his paper*): error number one, concerning the material being:

MERCY: We are neither fresh nor newly bathed, since there's not a drop of water in the whole town and we merely wiped ourselves with a rag dipped in alcohol. On the other hand, our dazzling wigs, which all are admiring as they ought, are not salmon colored as in the naive appraisal you have uttered, but rather grated carrot color, which is not the same.

HELP: Error number two, concerning the material peripheral being:

CLEMENCY: It is neither Camels, a cigarette we loathe for its verbal allusion known to us all and which reminds us of the nickname of our childhood, nor is it Shoulton Old Spice, but rather Fleur de Racaille de Caron: *en perfumes on sait très bien à quel saint se vouer.*

HELP: Error number three, concerning the phrasing of the insult and propriety in the use of words, since each one, as we know, has its own meaning—which is what excludes all synonymy—and this can neither be changed nor transferred.

MERCY: In fact, it has nothing to do with a fratricide, since no kindred ties us to the one you believed torn to pieces; we have not perpetrated it, we shall simply be the "intellectual authors," and, on the other hand, the adjectives bloodcurdling, ignoble, belong to a past aesthetic...but let's not enter into details.

HELP (*radio announcer, angel of the apocalypse with a tenor sax, entangled in bunches of ribbons, haloed, barefoot on a sword*): And lastly, the fourth error, the least forgivable, concerning the spiral quality of the time of the being:

CLEMENCY: The famous crime, the fratricide of which you speak, in spite of having been the theme of line number two, we now being on three, has not yet taken place. It would be inane to think that the numerical order corresponds to the time sequence; that is, we have not yet revealed anything, the senator to whom Dolores's destiny will be bound has not yet appeared, since in this meeting he announces his aspiration to be councilman. Lastly, even if this had taken place after Dolores's death, we would not have celebrated by coming to a meeting, but instead would have remained close to her body.

NARRATOR TWO: Well then, what the hell are you doing here?

HELP, MERCY, CLEMENCY: The same as always—that is—taking care of Dolores—faithful and eternal as we are—moral support—lads-in-waiting—etc., etc.

NARRATOR TWO: Ah, then Dolores is coming to the meeting?

HELP: She's coming, but not exactly to complain, like us, about the lack of water, indeed not to make any complaint at all; she's coming simply because the Spaniard promised (in line one, since that one does take place before this moment, and just before)

NARRATOR TWO: And the spiral?

HELP (*without answering him, looks out of the corner of his eye, which is elongated by a golden line*): if he wins the election for councilman which of course will happen, in order for the poem to come true step by step (*which is already beginning to bore us*), and without obstacles (*for which I beseech you end this line right now*)

NARRATOR ONE: It shall be done in a few lines.

HELP: to take her to Camagüey, and what's more, if we understand correctly (since, in parenthesis, that damn peninsular accent is a pain in the neck), he promised that once there, he was going to ask for her hand, since he can't mean cut off her hand as far as we know since it has nothing to do with the cutting off of hands as with delinquent slaves, which she isn't. So that. But let's finish.

NARRATOR TWO: Dolores, there she is!

DOLORES (*puffing, from all that running*): What a trip, holy cow! Bouncing like the dancing turkey in the circus on an electric iron! I've been bounced around in a tobacco cart drawn by two oxen over hill and dale, night and day, but I've finally arrived. And it's worth it. I'm the first, the founder of Mortal's Fan Club. I'll have six hundred pictures of him in my room, a lock of his blond hair in a locket. (*And changing her tone.*) Boy, am I hungry. Anybody have a sandwich for me?

NARRATOR ONE: Nobody, Nobody. No cheese for Jerry. Not even a scrap of ham for Tom. Tens of thousands like you have come. From the most out-of-the-way places. Haitians and Jamaicans in railway caravans. Singing and leaping from car to car, on sacks of white sugar. The trains like wakes of fire in the night, whistling, repeating Mor-tal-Pé-rez!

MORTAL (*in complete possession of the microphones and the public, under a rain of purple lampoons*): There'll be more than you've seen since the Deluge!

(*Last applause and cheers. Help, Mercy, and Clemency demand improvements, pinch each other, take off their eyebrows and prick each other. The dog passes by again.*)

HELP, MERCY, CLEMENCY: Water! Water! Water! (*And they squirm and do somersaults in the sand, they swallow red stones and slobber, the thirsty things—they think they see turrets, an oasis.*)

On Where Lies True Grandeur _____

At Dolores's house

NARRATOR ONE (*shaking a maraca*): He won! He won!

NARRATOR TWO (*does a somersault, falls off the hammock*): What' s up?

NARRATOR ONE: Oh, I woke you up. It's just that I'm a little ahead of time. We have to shout in a few lines, at a party.

NARRATOR TWO: Are we going to a party? What about destiny? And Dolores?

NARRATOR ONE: Precisely, we've occupied all the previous lines pushing them aside with our empty talk, but since they are the essential theme of the poem we must make ourselves scarce.

NARRATOR TWO (*a bit scared*): What do you mean, make ourselves scarce? Not appear anymore?

NARRATOR ONE (*clarifying*): We will appear, yes, but as anonymous servant: hairdresser, dress designers, people who don't add up to being. As for the three Etruscan conductors of souls, who were yesterday a marvel...(*Without any transition: creole country dance. Guitars. The party people, the Matamoros trio arrive; rum with lemon. The sallow girls break their hips*)...are today Dolores's dressmaker, pastry cook and antique dealer: scissor, poison, and termite. (*The din approaches.*) Let's go! Now's when you have to shout! With feeling! Allegro vivace!

NARRATORS ONE and TWO (*allegro vivace*): He won! Mortal Pérez won!

DOLORES (*very lyrical*): Open doors and windows! The first to go are these shoes which were so tight on me, this shoulder bag, these pans. And now: bring in the water!

HELP: But honey, you know there's not a single drop in this damn town!

DOLORES: That's not the water I mean. Peroxide water: we're gonna be blonds!

MERCY: We're gonna be white!

HELP: We're gonna be pale!

CLEMENCY: Blond like corn, like light beer!

DOLORES: We got to pack. Yes, we're moving to a better house. In a fancy neighborhood. We're going to Camagüey, to Havana. In a sleeping-car suite. Call the

dressmaker, say it's Dolores Rondón calling… Dolores
Rondón…what a name for a council-man's wife…
Dolores de Pérez…Lola Pérez Rondón… There's
nothing you can do about it. We are the name we're
born with. (*In the party, someone steps on a dog; it howls.*)

MERCY: Here's the dressmaker!

DRESSMAKER (*who is Help in disguise. In her new metamorphosis, the Fate comes with enormous scissors, her head
shaved, like a mannikin, wearing a headband—a measur-
ing tape. Lines of black stitches run across her chest.*): Light
and Progress!

DOLORES: Oh, it seems to me I know you. Where have
we met before? Now I know: at the wake of…

DRESSMAKER (*takes a step back, to get her off the track*): Me
at a wake? Never. Chrysanthemums nauseate me,
candles make me choke, coffee attacks my liver, sleep-
less nights make me sallow, etcetera.

DOLORES: I must be wrong then. But let's talk about the
important things, about what they're wearing in Havana: we want bottle green silk, the kind of fur that
makes you cough, necklaces, gloves, hats with
flowers, and little birds and those sunglasses you can
see through without being seen.

DRESSMAKER: Like old crossbones!

DOLORES: What?

DRESSMAKER: Like the cross-eyed, who cover their eyes,
but they see, they keep seeing, they see too much.

DOLORES: Oh, right. (*shouting*) Hey what's happening,
isn't there anything to drink in this house? A daiquiri
for the dressmaker!

(*Cheers to victory, to* MORTAL.)

Pride and Arrogance

In the capital of the province

HAIRDRESSER: There must be method to your madness. There must be method. Change lovers, Dolores. Hair color. Houses. But not gods. Your speaking high-class and not mumbling like a councilman's wife should, putting in two gold teeth for pure show and without ever having had the slightest toothache, drinking scotch on the rocks and Tom Collinses, pretending to be blind so as not to recognize your friends, going to bed with your blond servants, abandoning the poor Spaniard to the dizzying heights of the mayor's office, where, as everybody knows, he follows your advice and recruits an army of mambo dancers in your image and likeness from the farthest corners of the province…all this is permitted. All of it. But there must be method. You must keep up the appearance of method. There must be method within the lack of method. I'm tripping on my words. I mean that you mustn't forget the glass of water, the sunflowers, the roosters. I mean you mustn't forget the offerings to the gods.

DOLORES (*with her head in a plastic dryer. Operatic. With pride and arrogance.*): What's with the servants? First that old bag the antique dealer snickering at me, all because I asked for twisted chairs and a Simmons mattress. Then toad eyes, the housekeeper, who didn't recognize me in a two-piece suit. Then the pastry cook with her rice pudding (*and on a long high note*); I want

73

a Banana Split! And now you, the Attila of hairdress-
ing, after mangling my tresses, my beautiful straight
hair, my skull, my whole head; after applying stinking pomades to straighten it, electric dryers to curl it,
massages to straighten it again, curling irons; after
leaving me scabby, scalped, bald as an egg...now it's
method. Now it's saints. Now that they're preparing
another banquet, another candidacy, another
partyswitching, another caucus (*she's complaining, the
poor thing*)...How much further, Catalina, will you
carry the abuse of our forbearance? Madness, Method.
Loaded words. Which of the two has the bigger
mouth? Which swallows the other? Does madness
swallow, digest, expel method? Does method gag on
madness? Do both devour, fear, flee each other? I don't
know. I only know that the kitchen pots are under
the bed and the chamber pots on the stove. That's
the method. I only know that you've left me bald.

THE HAIRDRESSER (*almost crying*): No, Dolores. You've
had too much to drink. Bloody Marys unhinge you.
It's not true about your hair. We straightened it, we
made it blond and purple like a piece of cloud, then
we turned it into flames. You weren't satisfied. You
wanted concentric ringlets, upside-down towers, ship
prows. You wanted a Flavian hair style. You said: "I
am Titi." Hence the aluminum dryers, the high voltage, the muriatic acids, the curling iron, the stench.
That's the way of method. You wanted to be a bird, a
gazelle, you loathed your slanty eyes. Hence the spin-
ach mascara, the baby pineapple cream, the simulta-
neous massages, and the Helena Rubin-stein beauty

sunfluid. We did what we could. That's the way of method. The well-rounded, clean, classified, filed, alphabetically ordered way, in the belly of method. That's how it is.

DOLORES (*Valkyric*): No! You won't stop me, you won't tie me down like a goat. If you don't change, you get stuck. I'll keep moving ahead, always ahead, like a train. This very day I'll pack my bags. I'm going. From here to Havana. This dusty city without ships, I without Chinese restaurants, I can't stand it any longer. I want chop suey, fried rice, chicken with almonds, glazed pork. I'll go wherever the wind takes me. To Peking, to Hong Kong. Bald as you've left me. Cross-eyed, lame: no matter what, I'll reach my destiny on time, like an American train. Life is a soap dish; if you don't fall, you slip. I'm going. We'll win the municipal, provincial, senatorial, national elections. I'll be the wife of a senator. I'll have more and more admirers: That's Hip Power for you!

And to you, servants who refuse to follow me, who despise victory, who want to stay buried here like the snake in its cave, to you I leave these blond pieces of straw, my last hairs, those wires you've twisted over my head; you who despise the capital, the swell life,

POWER AND PROMINENCE

you who in the eleventh hour abandon me, in the hour of the great election, the soya beans, and the egg roll, I free you of job and wages. Faithful, the only among a whole staff of boisterous, demanding, angry, irritated, and mad servants, my three advisors follow me: the dressmaker, pastry cook, and antique dealer. The elegance, and sweetness, of past and present. Three sacrificing souls. At least there'll be pastries, frozen meringues, and Mandarin oranges. I'm going to the ships. Bald, lame, but to Havana.

(*The drumming of typewriters. Traffic lights. Ships. Sirens fading in and out.*)

NARRATOR ONE: Do you hear it? Havana. She wanted it, she herself hastens her own destiny, jumps toward it like a fish toward the shore. She wants Havana, she wants the swell life, she wants, as she says, to imitate our illustrious Cuban classic, the adventurous Countess of Merlin. Well here is the beginning of the end: here's Havana!

DOLORES (*with the emphasis of all political apotheosis*): Faithful servants, dear shadows of myself. Let's begin the senatorial stage with a bang. I knew I'd be a senator's wife. There are the votes, there is Mortal acclaimed by the caucuses, the parties, the people themselves! The days of the province, the dust, the rooster, are way behind us. The bathtub. I want a bath. A bathtub full of rum. And then they can fan me with giant leaves. This is the life the four of us deserve. Today we'll throw gold coins to the little black boys! Bring the wig, the tightest corset, the spangle, the orchid that arrived this morning from Miami. I'm going to the Presidential Palace! (*The telephone rings.*)

THE DRESSMAKER (*answering the phone*): She's not in, Mrs. Senator is not in! (*She snickers, hangs up with a bang.*)

NARRATOR TWO (*remorseful*): You got to admit it. Dolores
has reached her baroque period. She's outdoing herself, beating her own record. This is all going to end
like a Chinaman's spree. Her reading has done her a
lot of damage. It's driven her insane. It's okay for her
to learn English, which, in parenthesis, she speaks like
a Haitian; it's okay for her to order perfumes and frozen flowers from Miami, but the Cuban classics have
been the strongest of all. What digestion. There she
is, having herself fanned by two fat Negresses after a
rum bath. Just like the "Countess of Berlin," she says.
Good God!

All Is Bound to Perish

(*The telephone rings.*)

THE ANTIQUE DEALER (*who, naturally, is a mutation of
Clemency. Lying on llama skin, tightly fitted in pink and
gold silk—the tail of her dress looks like a flower vase—
hair in an upsweep with Cuban floral motifs. In her hand
a modern style telephone; the receiver is a horn painted by
an Ethiopian primitive.*): Mrs. Senator is not in, away
on presidential business. (*But oh, they have terrible news
for her.*) What? That's impossible! (*She jumps up—and
breaks a heel. How pale she has become!*) No! (*She screams.
The other two Fates draw near and scream too: wails of
woe, gnashing of teeth, howls that unhinge the earth.*)

NARRATOR TWO (*at his wit's end*): What's happening?

NARRATOR ONE (*biblical, with a silvery, curling patriar-
chal beard, the tablets of the Law in his hands*): What had

to happen. Do you remember the parable of the animals?

NARRATOR TWO: Of course I remember, but stop pestering me with your parables. What's happening at Dolores's house? What hell is breaking loose? What gods have come with the banner of death?

NARRATOR ONE (*unperturbed*): We'll get to that. Let's begin with the Cycle of Zoophagy: toads eat flies, snakes eat toads, bulls eat snakes, men eat bulls. Here's the explanation. This morning, at five. Stifling heat in the presidential suite. Eroticisms. Drinks. Etcetera. Sex changes for obvious reasons. Number one: women eat bulls. Well then, the dancer called "The Girl with the Diamond in Her Navel," (*and here the spent mirrors, neon flowers, background curtain with gondolas, and Ravel's* Bolero, *the trademark of every striptease.*)

PRESIDENT: Enough of those Tahitian dances! That navel going around and around, making circles, opening and closing like Cyclops' eye, that navel, I tell you, is making me cockeyed, I'm getting seasick. I see it going around and around by itself, like a spinning top.

DANSEUSE: A fine homage, for someone like me who's squandered so much of her international talent here.

PRESIDENT: And I my pesos to see Camagüeyen hips.

DANSEUSE: Which I've sure suffered for. And are they stuck to your wallet? A "special performance" at the Palace. That's what they promised me. A performance with lights and color posters. I see myself stuck here and I can't believe it. No public, no bravos, no orchids in the dressing room, no telegrams. Reduced to a room and a bed. I who gave up everything to come. I, wanted at the Negresco of Paris, the Lido of Rome. I, the most sought-after, the "assoluta," the girl with the wiggly hips. Somebody's gonna pay for this!

PRESIDENT: You misread the tourist pamphlets. Business is bad. A bad beginning makes a bad ending.

DANSEUSE: You're in for a bad ending and your gang is too. I, goddess of Papeete, here with my jewels. Among crooks. I who gilded my eyelids à la Cleopatra for the palace spotlights, and bought myself a dress, a three-string necklace, a grated carrot with asparagus cream-colored wig; I who invented a "pleasing and presidential number," like Madam Rondón told me. They're all in for a bad ending. They are a bad ending.

PRESIDENT: Get out of here, zombie. Plumed serpent.

DANSEUSE: You'd do better to say Goddess of Liberty!

NARRATOR ONE (*the music stops*): And that's how the zoophagous cycle starts. Women eat bulls. Funny, isn't it? And the bull, what does he do?

NARRATOR TWO: He eats the snake.

NARRATOR ONE: Of course. The President, outraged, flies like a bat out of hell to the serpent, who is the prime minister. The reptile is sleeping, but the first magistrate awakens him with insults, since it was he who obtained, also imported, like I was saying, the liquor, drugs, and danseuse. It is, to keep track of chronologies and order, six in the morning and we are in the second stage.

NARRATOR TWO: How horrible! Each phrase of yours, which seemed banal and gratuitous, takes on great

79

meaning, becomes part of a clockwork machinery. How great you are, author of Dolores Rondón!

NARRATOR ONE: Save your praise for the end. It is seven A.M.: the serpent is about to devour the toad. Listen:

PRIME MINISTER: You wretch, you bastard. To have sent me that revolting courtesan. That Camagüeyan tramp pretending she was an exquisite dancer from Hawaii. Look what's happened! It's all over! Don't you ever dare set foot in the Capitol building or the House again!

SECRETARY TO THE PRIME MINISTER: But my dear sir, don't get confused, don't get excited, remember the heart cannot be replaced. Our dear friend Mortal Pérez introduced me to her, she was taken from the "Army of Art" in Camagüey, her native land.

NARRATOR TWO (*cries*): Now I understand. Poor Dolores.

NARRATOR ONE: Let us keep our cold objectivity till the end. This morning at eight, while Dolores was taking her rum bath, Mortal was publicly accused of white slavery, drug smuggling, importing liquor illegally, an attempt against public morality, traitor to the party, atheist, etc.... and he has been declared persona non grata.

(*Holding hands, slow, weightless, the Fates revolve. Their pearly feet barely touch the floor. Their hair floating. Underwater opaqueness. Their screams reach us fragmented, broken.*)

DOLORES (*with a tragic sense of existence*): Earth swallow me! Earth swallow me! Earth swallow me!

THE DRESSMAKER: All tragedy is repetitive!

THE PASTRY COOK (*a candied metamorphosis of Mercy. Bal-*

ancing on her head a tray topped with honeyed grapefruits, napoleons, fruitcakes, rum cakes): All repetition is rhetorical!

DOLORES: Yes, earth that witnessed my birth, open now, eat me, dissolve me, turn me to stone! What fury in the saints! What a fire in my head! Servants, if you're still there, if you still haven't carried off the furniture and curtains, bring me a bag of ice and lemonade. How can I pacify the saints now? How can I go back in time, change the course of events? Ice! Fans! What a fire!

THE DRESSMAKER: Here we are, faithful servants.

THE PASTRY COOK: We are following you. We are watching your every step. We were your shadow in the full glare of day, now we will lead you into darkness.

THE DRESSMAKER: Here you are, madam. A mango milk shake. Take with ice and brown sugar the fruit you denied the gods and which they no longer accept from you. Take it.

DOLORES (*as carefree as if she were at a canasta party*): Oh, how delicious! How nice and sweet! Real Philippine mangos! We're lucky, all things considered, we still have the blender! (*And returning to Tragedy.*) Look at me Camagüeyans, sons of the flattest province, the mountainless, the land of the labyrinth of the Twelve Leagues and the Isles and Islets of the Queen; look at me, glorious lineage of cattle!

THE DRESSMAKER (*recitative*): And of the water jars filled with toads!

THE ANTIQUE DEALER (*recitative*): And of the mystical verse makers!

DOLORES: Look at the end of my career. I leave what I have. Nothing is left except what I have given away. Look at my house: the servants abandon their posts and flee, rats from a sinking ship, ants from a flooded cave; the creditors surround us. I leave it all. I part without regrets. (*In the canasta-party tone again.*) My, that was good! Is there more? (*And tragic again.*) Let the heavens break over me! Mortal is already arriving by the service stairway, hiding, as if infected with the plague, crying, his feet swollen.

MORTAL: What a pain in my feet! What grief! (*The Fates cry, snip each other's hair with scissors, cover the mirrors with black cloths.*) Quiet! I don't want any weeping, just a basin of hot water, a place to put these growing, swelling feet.

THE DRESSMAKER: Oh Mortal, what's to become of us?

THE PASTRY COOK: For whom shall we cook the pork and beans now, for whom the Spanish dishes and diction, for whom the door-to-door vote buying?

THE ANTIQUE DEALER: And God's compassionate eye, and the Valencian paella, will they return no more?

THE DRESSMAKER: Feel better now, sir?

MORTAL (*sighing*): Yes, it's easing up already. I walked too much...

THE PASTRY COOK: And there's still more to go!

NARRATOR ONE: So, we reach the final stage, the last judgment: Dolores steps out of her bath and sees Mortal, barefoot, with his feet on the dining-room table, one of the last pieces of furniture left. The Fates take the basin of hot water and slender, slow, graceful, they dance to the window and throw it to the street.

(*Predictable symmetry! The basin, upon falling, repeats the sound we heard when, in the euphoria of electoral success, Dolores threw her pots and pans out the window.*)

_____ And You Only Immortalize

DOLORES (*lento, ma non troppo*): How great you are, Nothingness! How boundless! You, the unique: a god with neither feet nor head. To you my life, still river. City without walls. I walk. The towers do not retreat. This empty square, this silence, are the same as before; this night in which I return to the point of departure and again turn into dust and poverty, this night in which I wait is again the same impatient night of my departure, my eyes as watchful as then, the offerings ready on the cabinet, a fruit before each saint. At that time I asked the four roads to open before me. I left early. Without baggage. Just as I come back. The water has not moved. The tower does not retreat.

HELP: While the others sleep, she keeps watch.

MERCY: While they sing and shout, she keeps quiet.

CLEMENCY: While they eat and drink, she fasts.

HELP: Come on Dolores! What's past is past. Power is past. The day is past. The whole city sleeps. There's not a sound in the square; we can hear the flies flying in this crummy hotel you've ended up in, across the street

from the station. They're all sleeping, snoring away.
Mouths agape. Sweating. Naked in their hammocks.
Rocking. On the floor. Among empty bottles. Having
sweet dreams.

DOLORES: I keep watch.

CLEMENCY: The flowers upon the rosemary spray
Young Maid may school thy sorrow
The blue-eyed flower that blooms today
To honey turns tomorrow.

Come sing, Dolores! And buy us a drink, like you bought
us one the very night you waited for Mortal, to run
away. Come down to the dance. Do not fear symmetry. The dancers, the *danzón,* the pianola, are waiting
for you.

DOLORES: I keep quiet.

MERCY: To your health, Dolores. Come to the banquet.
To the great stuffed pig. Stuffed with tender wild pigeons stuffed with flowers. They're all eating. They
eat and vomit and eat again. Don't miss out on the
young pig, the rosy suckling roasted among guayaba
leaves, he looks like a baby! Dinner is ready. Hallelu-
jah!

DOLORES: I fast.

Here I waited one night. The same dust, the same
square, Mortal was coming in the morning. We were
on our way to wealth and power. Nothing changed.
The province stands still. But I have one joy left: the
sight of your sleeping face, God, waiting for you to
wake up, staying here, fixed before you, looking at
you. Of myself I leave a testimony: my life written on
a stone, by my tomb. No one will read it but the beg-

gars, the gravediggers, and the windows, no one will touch it but the lizards and the red bramble, or perhaps the black couples who make love on the cool grass of the cemetery, fearless, offering life to death. I leave you these words so that you'll remember me, my life in ten lines, in marble, so that neither rain nor wind will erase it:

> Dolores Rondón did here
> reach the end of her career,
> come, mortal, and ponder
> on where lies true grandeur.
> Pride and arrogance,
> power and prominence,
> all is bound to perish.
> And you only immortalize
> the evil you economize
> and the good you may cherish.

The Evil You Economize

The province, before Mortal's election

DOLORES: Brothers.
BABALAO ONE: Come in.
DOLORES: I come about a dream.
BABALAO TWO: Speak.
BABALAO ONE: What did you see?
DOLORES: A banquet.
BABALAO ONE: What dishes?

DOLORES: Roast suckling pig, yellow rice, and cocoanuts.

BABALAO ONE: Very good they seem.

BABALAO TWO: Elegua's favorites.

DOLORES: I saw more.

BABALAO TWO: Tell us.

DOLORES: I saw the guests, white people. And I saw parakeets of every color around the table, talking, and in the middle of the table a large covered bowl.

BABALAO ONE: And inside?

DOLORES: All the guests sit down merrily amidst the hubbub of the parrots, I uncover the big bowl and inside I see a toad, all swollen as if it were about to burst, with red popping eyes like a rabbit's. And when I put the cover upside down on the table, inside, around its edge, a black snake.

BABALAO ONE: Holy Spirit!

BABALAO TWO: Let us see.

(They throw conch shells on a mat.)

BABALAO ONE: Let the flowers of stone, let the eyes of the sea tell us.

BABALAO TWO: They say this: you will find a white man who talks a lot and in a fine manner. The gold and the tablecloths come with him. But stay there. Do not wish for more. Be careful. Be sure to make your daily offering, be sure not to offend the gods. Do not disown them. They are like dogs, they go away if they do not recognize the master's hand.

BABALAO ONE: And they ask for the flower that revolves like them. And honey.

DOLORES: They shall be given.

BABALAO ONE: Good days are ahead. And after, a sword.

DOLORES: God forbid.

BABALAO ONE: Stop in time. No ambitions. Make your offerings. Stop in time.

DOLORES: But where? Which time is that?

BABALAO ONE: That they do not know. Or do not want to know.

DOLORES: I don't understand.

BABALAO ONE: That's all they say.

DOLORES: After all it's just a dream. And these, a couple of shells.

BABALAO ONE: Nothing but a dream.

DOLORES: And stones.

_____ And the Good You May Cherish

The province, shortly after the fall

NARRATOR ONE: We're already on the last line! All the themes must be caught, tied and untied, sewn, paired, mixed, slid over each other, with melodious sounds, guts full of wind.

NARRATOR TWO: May the meritorious Writers Guild be on our side!

HELP (*orthophonic*): D. Frontal O. Liquid L. Posterior O. R. E. Sibilant S. Do-lo-res.

MERCY: Do-la-res.

CLEMENCY: There is only one letter of difference between the two. Only one. The letter on a money order from the Holy Mother's Vault in the Royal Bank of Canada. Dolores makes dolares!

NARRATOR TWO: Take advantage. Attack the main theme.

NARRATOR ONE (*is a radio announcer, as if he were advertising toothpaste*): Yes, ladies and gentlemen, as you see, the ring master, the prime mover is still the pun, the double somersault. Thus we lose the essential: the word runs before the game as the dog before the slicing machine. He sees the sausages in him. In slices, with olives, in a sandwich…and he runs off. He runs off barking and, the saying says it, his bark is worse than his bite. Hence so many barking…but toothless, words.

DOLORES (*despondent*): Nothing is left!

HELP: Something is left. Dollars are left. We know. Your bank account is full of zeros. Come on, don't put on the poor act. Write us a check. A pretty pink one.

MERCY: We want a mamey milk shake, mamey-colored silk shirts, black and white slacks, little hats. Dark green dollars!

DOLORES: No more account. No more career. No more fat cows, they're consumptive, dehydrated, the widows of bulls, dissolved into dirt.

NARRATOR TWO: Another unhinged zoology!

NARRATOR ONE: You who said that all was useful, that all served some purpose. This is a fine situation for you. Tell me what purpose this chain devourment has, is, serving, what purpose Dolores Rondón's life serves, what purpose her death will serve. Has "behavior" been "modified"? Have the "essences" been "grasped"? Nothingness. Delicious Nothingness milk shake.

HELP (*dodecaphonic*): Where there once was fire, ashes remain!

MERCY (*baroque*): A powerful gentleman is Master Money!

CLEMENCY (*rapid requiem*): What an emetic!

DOLORES (*Dolorosa in a sacramental act*): These are the only pesos left. The last of them. For the light and water bills. Take them.

HELP (*in Duke Ellington jazz, Duke at the piano, Cootie Williams on trumpet, Ray Nance, violin, Chuck Connors, bass trombone, etc.*): We will be showing out-of-this-world originals...

NARRATOR ONE (*repetitive and obsessive*): As if all this would penetrate some thick skull, entertain some...

MERCY (*in bossa nova*): By Schiaparelli, Chanel, and Christian Dior...

NARRATOR TWO (*furious*): Driveling reader slumped in his chair before the soporific stew of everyday living!

CLEMENCY (*like Eartha Kitt on a gilded* récamier, *extremely feline*): And we will use exclusivité perfumes...

NARRATOR ONE: Those are the four parts that united, the essences!

NARRATOR TWO: How ontic!

HELP (*who is Ella Fitzgerald*): From the Maison Rocha!

NARRATOR ONE: All has a purpose, all is final, all returns to all.

DOLORES: That is, to nothing.

NARRATOR TWO: To nothing.

HELP, MERCY, CLEMENCY (*emblematic and signaletic*): Right!

(*Chord on a guitar.*)

THE ENTRY OF CHRIST IN HAVANA

"The serpent, the emerald clarity, I saw it by my head, splattering vinegar; but not Mortal, not even his footsteps in the dust I swallow searching for him, in the stones that cut my feet, in the red bramble. Of what did he drink? Of the pasture of what animals has he eaten? Did thirst kill him? Turn his bones to ashes? Dry his throat and eyes? Are they the ones that look at me, burnt, ashen, flanked with threads of blood? Is this the promised orchard, this absence of trees, this gnashing of teeth?"

Mercy could see herself finding him, draped in damasks, carrying her bleeding breasts on a tray. She saw herself as an infanta, flower of Aragon, open-winged plateresque bird, fixed among apples and snakes from Flemish tapestries, on her head the felt miter, the cardinal's hat of worsted tassels, the three-cornered hat, the round and octagonal gold hat; tattoed in Mudéjar borders, engraved in the heraldic purple of the Courts, written in the sky of an engraving among masts and contorted angels, pointing toward the port of Cadiz. She dreamed her face was deformed by the churrigueresque style, by provincial woodworks, by a rock garden reflected in the volute of a mimbar. She imagined herself, the poor thing, leaving the Palace of Two Waters, bent under the weight of crackling jewels, the pace of her sorrel horse punctuated by a band of Moroccan tambourines, convoyed by Indians, yes, Indians with Brazilian parakeets, baskets of tobacco and sugar cane. She even sniffed the nearby scent of brown sugar, and of the black sweat she tasted with her fingertip, an expert sampler, and of aguardiente and rotten orchids.

That's what Mercy wanted to be, conqueror of Mortal and the world, a new Cid, bastion of Castille, Inquisitor of the Mohammedans and the circumcised; she wanted to cross the Manchegan dust again, galloping over broken turrets with a drove of steeds, swaying baroque incensories over shit-stained Korans, founding monasteries, beheading Almoravide princes, then washing herself with holy water.

..."He would travel in the morning. The branches would sprinkle dewdrops upon his horse's mane, and would hide the sun from him as he proceeded, letting through only the necessary light. The growing clarity sowed pieces of gold in his clothing, elusive to his fingers. There were fruits so full and of such delicate skin, that they seemed like liqueurs waiting to be imbibed without the need of a glass, and there were running waters where pebbles crackled like jewels in the hands of beautiful women..."[1]

---

1 Adaptation of a poem by Mutanabbí (915 – 965) *wafir, nun,* number 175, translated by Emilio García Gómez.

It didn't last long. Of little use were so many gold trinkets. Banners and rumpled rags, mitered and scabby heads: they all rot. Whose stench is it? Who tilts the scale of the vanities? On one plate of the balance, the dried, bald heads of Help and Mercy, crowning the diadems that once crowned them; on the other their bibles and viscera. Who will save them? Who's the highest bidder? Going through his Mansions, searching for Mortal dead or alive, pregnant with him, so did the Faithful fall on the Sierra of Ronda, so did the pistol shots surprise them, the cracking of Toledan swords clearing the way, the hoarse "hands up" of the bandits and hands pawing their hips, the smell of men and wine.

They defended themselves with their nails. They waved papal bulls and amulets in their faces. The blasphemers' thirst was greater. Now they're rolling on the ground, two-bit whores, courtesans for a glass of sangria, their cheeks bitten, their shoulders tattooed with enemy coats of arms. Swinging their hips they go, flamenco dancing in the farmhouses, dragging their Saint Theresa sandals, yes, with those dried and porous nougat faces, and wine-flushed eyes, bent over their nags like harassed picadors, dragging, downtrodden Easter Virgins with their false gold trinkets.

In spite of those spites they want to dance. They shout "I have the blood of kings in the palm of my hand!" and they tap their heels again and again. But they yawn. The guitars are out of tune. They fall out of step. Remain nailed to the platform. Get rings under their eyes. Cramps. They sweat. Their eyes go dry on them, and then they see by their heads a serpent, an emerald clarity.

Threadbare Virgins? Never! They retrieve their money

(but their honor, oh no!—they say). Under those rags they wear silks, that pregnancy has been girdled by wide sashes, and they bear the signatures of Cordoban silversmiths on forged bracelets, lockets of saints' bones, charms that Mortal once wore, coffer to keep his locks in. Do you feel sorry for them, wearing the common wide hats of ruffians and muleteers? Well, underneath are turbans that are jugs of doubloons and, of the sandals, the double sole is a genealogical tree of repoussé leather. Yes, they wear their ancestry on their feet, the gaudy things; they step on the grapevines of more than one crown:

That wine made viceroyships of provinces, ennobled generations of dealers and slave drivers. They search for an impossible, it's true, but they travel equipped for anything. They peddle advertisements for gambling houses and beehives—the brothels of Malaga—; in those cells, Apocryphal beggars, fortune-tellers, procuresses bribe black princesses, houris of Magreb harems, badly castrated eunuchs who answer them with their contralto voices:

HELP and MERCY (*hands clasped, eyes turned toward the sky—and in them the cross reflected, of course*): Sad hermaphrodites, by the law of contrasts you must know of him, he slept in these beds, did you not wash his private parts in the ablutions of before and after the act, did you not kiss the rings on his feet, anoint his chest with holy oils and cinnamon, perfume the air, as he passed, with jasmine pomegranates?

And the chorus of paint-smeared fat men answers moaning over the orange-studded crowns, rending their white cloaks.

THE CHORUS (*the languid sopranos in their cells, accompa-*

nied by cymbals): Yes! We saw him twice, twice did he honor our beds. We tasted of his juice and today we felt his thirst more inextinguishable than the *ayma*;[2] he tempered us like guitars, filled our cups...he left for Córdoba, he left for Medina, he stayed, all at once, because he is everywhere!

The Wait in Medina-Az-Zahara[3]

Not capitals, but wooden caps perforated with Koranic letters; the tortoise shell of the texts appears once and again around those heads like the small animals in a Zirí dynasty plate, forming praises and precepts, and from those star-shaped symmetries a jet-black foliage descends—the matted hair of the Moorish Mademoiselles—twisted around the marble columns of their bodies. At their feet, a still river, the blue dust that was once paved with ponds and fountains. In it, water within water, the Azahara had dissolved.

That murmur of cisterns now belongs to the growing bramble; that dampness, an orange glow, levitates over the ground: a garden which the sun duplicates and evaporates; those terraces, cellars, their celebrations, mournings.

Help and Mercy bend down to listen: nothing, not even

---

2 A thirst, which the ancient Arabs had, for she-camel milk.

3 Medina-Az-Zahara, near Córdoba, palace built in 936 by Adb Er Rahma Anasir III for his favorite Azahara.

the birds have remained. So do the Veiled and Vigilant spend day and night at the ruins, waiting.

"Waiting is to become nothing"—they hum from time to time, and over their quartered bodies they let serpents creep. They are salamanders, sweet vermin; they offer that stillness to Mortal.

They neither eat, nor drink, nor join their stiffened eyelids. They decipher the neighboring capitals and from that reading receive omens of The Arrival and patience. Then they smile with their floury cracks, move their pupils of white and pink radii, and think that the joyful day is near.

So passes a time that has neither direction nor measure, until a crew of excavators approaches the palace. Stucco ruins, someone points out, and they crumble. From that rubbish, dusting themselves, two lady wildcat and bible vendors step out. Again they arouse the peasants' surprise, standing there in the middle of the chorus, frozen in speechmaking poses; in their baskets, felines battle among psalms.

"Not for these rough stones, oh peasants, nor for archeological treasure whatsoever did we come; but rather for signs of our lord. You look for empty palaces; we a king who deserves them. The stones are already ascending. Pray tell us if near them he has passed. His name is Mortal and "he wears the celestial robe from the looms of Almería."[4]

The Sancho Panzas want to mount their horses and

4 Verse from Ben Guzmán, twelfth century.

In a Dream _____

Questioning, the Majas jump up and down in front of the foreman. Carriers of banderillas, they wave them like double piccolos and extricate their little feet from the ground, crossing them, striking first one hip then the other with them, dancers of the Aragonese jota. Are they going to hurl a javelin? No, they run, jump, touch each other in air; the crack is that of two small mildewed plates, or of a tambourine full of water.

The foreman wants to catch them and runs below, his hands open, awkward sunflowers, following the route of the Skilled Ones.

The Dog Heads picture themselves: in levitation, disarrayed angels, made of striated cubes, heads on backward, false tresses—tiaras of stones and sticks—falling, gold in gold, in a goblet which they raise between their hands. An indigo cloth covers them and on it, concentric creases, elbows and knees are insinuated. These touch (and cross), because the Princesses are two mountebanks, and the ground the letters of the gospel.

The foreman, way below, bearded, following them with his eyes, throwing pieces of earthen jugs at them to make them trip and fall, yes, they see him with half-moon horns, lanceolated ears and a tail of black bristles wagging in the air (not to mention the other, that exposed and over-flowing earthen vessel); he drools, he wants to lick their feet.

They, naked intertwined herons over a plate of grapes and laurels, nailed upon a wooden heraldry, in red on the white half, in Prussian blue on the feathered half.

Help and Mercy were sleeping on a pallet, among bull

and satyr heads, knees, volutes of Corinthian capitals and pieces of Omeyan plates. So did day discover the rubble and aforementioned plate of grapes, and the foreman the other giver of fire, their bodies sweetly naked under the sheets. It is true that, as in the dream, he licked their feet. He drank of them. He left on their breasts a smell of olives. They awoke damp and startled. Help shouted: "rascals, scoundrels, satyrs." And Mercy: "heretics, fiends." They leapt from the cushions, and not to the dust but to a carpet which covered it. Where the foreman had left the trace of his calloused feet when, playing the innocent, he came to them.

"Here, oh chaste mothers, is this souvenir (*and he pointed to the carpet with a king-of-hearts gesture*), a sign of Mortal's stay here that he left before he moved on. Give it to them—he said to me—so that they will love it as they love me." (And he turned dancingly on his heel.) Let it not surprise us then that the Fat Heads, still naked, parade the carpet among the ruins. They caress it, yes, they offer it raisins, fresh cheese, and goat's milk, they stand in front of it so that the sun won't fade it, they call it "banner," or "godgiven," or "burnt water."

HELP (*yawning*): Mortal thought of our honor: a carpet to carpet us. Sold, it would make our fortune, pawned, our bed and board, traded to the looms of Almería, our heaviest jewel.

MERCY (*who perfumed it with incense*): Shut up, magpie, potbelly. Giving it to you is like throwing rare diamonds to swine. Fool, these threads of gold have meaning, Mortal's tongue is in them. A woven message; it cannot be taken for tatters.

Does Help wave hers? No. It's her laugh: little bones in a tumbler, sand dragged away by the river.

"You numbskull, you're stuffed with vulgar sayings. Nothing says nothing. Let's sell it quickly, or it will be coveted by bandits and rats. Dust comes to dust. Water rots the threads."

"Those threads of your fate are already stinking, Sancha, Pot of Meatballs. Go away! Here's your part. Finish it off in pork and beans."

The scissor grates, bites the plush along the middle, as it does the fate of the Pale Ones. It's when the carpet is already cut that they look at each other, look again and immediately embrace in a jeremiad, howling. The unhappy creatures blow out their snot, riprap their clothes, bend over as if with stomach cramps, twitched into grimaces that cannot possibly disfigure them more than they are now. They're a lament, a breast-beating, a flamenco cry that doesn't stop.

"Look what we have done" (*and they pat each other on the back*).

"It was my fault. I, the transcendental, the fool" (Mercy).

"No, mine: the sweet tooth, never full" (Help).

And they hug and kiss. But it's too late.

Note: In the carpet, FAITH, a naked young woman (she covers one breast and her sex with her hands), hurries to enter the dining room, but already in front of the door, blocking her way, is EXPERIENCE, a hook-nosed and bilious old woman. Who in turn is stopped by a lazy round-faced page covered with a hat of feathers which open like lyres before the dried face of the old woman. The women whisper and nudge each other, relishing the banquet.

The blond prince has tasted the soup and is smiling. Under the table, between his legs, a frightened boy hides and two greyhounds play. The main dish, hog or wild boar meat, has been presented in a bowl in the shape of a ship, the sail is speckled skin and the wooden mast ends in a capital shaped like a pineapple. There are three lit tapers, goblets full of nuts, and a plate of open pomegranates.

(Mercy inquired into the meaning of the cloth. She unstitched it from the lining to see if it hid a written message; she only found the unraveled back of plates and heads: islands of knots, black stitches. The scar of the stitches traced another banquet in the canvas that was like a joke on the visible one, dull and full of clods. The plate of pomegranates was a dark green patch; the dinner guests cross-eyed puppets. Next to the border a left hand pointed to a striated piece of material, separated from the rest.

Tearful Mercy resewed the carpet, pricking her fingers.)

A dark young man, HICCUPS, turns down the splendid food and gives orders to the band. Which consists of three flutists with puffed cheeks, a mandolin, harp, and drum. The harpist, almost a dwarf, seems to be conducting the group. To his right the mandolin player bends his head under the weight of an abundantly convoluted turban, and to his left, the sad drummer tightens his muscles to hold up his instrument (a barrel with two leather skins and a chain) and press a perforated piccolo in his mouth.

Next to him another character (a musician) is showing

FAITH and EXPERIENCE something, but we can't see what it is, because there's a darning patch in its place.

MERCY

would redden stones with burning ash, and wait over the coals for dawn, like a thief in ambush. She would fast standing, in the dampest part of the cloister, repeat short prayers and Salve Reginas. She abandoned, for their leniency, her confessors and taking her half of the carpet (which she had unstitched again, interpreted according to numbers and stars, and made into the object of prayers), she spread it before a calvary, so that the faithful would step on it, and stain it with their scabs and tears.

She begged. She lived on bread and water. She suffered the hair shirt. She scourged herself. She drank bile and vinegar. She considered herself a strumpet and begged them to scorn her.

Her eyes sank into the back of her head from keeping watch at night, her feet were cracked from walking barefoot. She was reduced to mere bones. She lost her hair.

Note: By the right edge of the cloth, on a strip that feet had not profaned, remained an arm of the prince and the body of HICCUPS. A very pious little nun believed she saw in him our Lord. So she cut him off, framed him in a shroud, and hung him behind a door.

Help

What a smell of cinnamon! It's just that Help, along with cowbells and cowskulls, had placed fragrant timber among her tresses, certain that so much fragrance can only favor the sale. Although stiff, one would say that a hundred goats are grazing when she moves, such is the chiming of her tins. She comes wrapped in the merchandise: the purchase is the temptation to another more pleasureful one. In other words: she covers her nakedness with her half of the carpet, and apart from that, she wears only the tuneful hairdo.

So to the Palace she went. And lost both cloths: the brocade, and the one I leave to your imagination. She came out dressed, and if she was clinking, it was less from tin cans than from gold trinkets.

The marquis, who was a veteran, did not with this act do injustice to his past victories. Surprise did not unnerve him, and he consummated the conquest with the ritual chimings. When he finally sheathed his saber, they celebrated copiously with aged wines.

Note: The carpet ended up in a winter dining room. Since the scissor snippings left the prince armless, the embroiderers decided to eliminate him and with him the floral border that framed three of the sides. They hung it among horns and rifles, on a wooden closet, sewn to a blue wreath with goats and *puttis*. They made bedspreads with the fringes; the body of the prince, the victim of two restorations, ended up in the garbage.

To Help _____

You came out laden with gold trinkets, but you quickly went downhill. You broke your incensory dancing the *pompompero*, your palms and heels grew calloused, you lost honor and hair. You dragged yourself, hide and bones, smeared white and carmine, down the roads of Fuengirolas like a beggarly holyman without once listening to a muezzin, or seeing the white of domes, or hearing any voice to break your fast. Your last shreds were spent on *manzanilla* and *anis del Mono*; you shuffled around, getting drunk in the holds of Magreb ships; at night you anointed yourself with perfumes and went out to wait for the harvesters. They left you their sweat, semen, and a few nickels. You returned with rings under your eyes, yellowed hair, bitten lips. You sang, you were an Arabian cantor with a great pink bow, a timbrel player; you pierced your graying pompom with an arrow of sparkles.

They called you Easy Francie, the Living-Dead. You couldn't even drag your own bones around anymore and you cursed Mortal, the carpet, and the day you were born; you were a hook-nosed and bilious old woman.

To Mercy _____

You deprived yourself of bracelets and of the honey crullers you so much liked; you gave up your veil for the stain and to the poor, your garments. You called yourself Ruin, Servant, you kissed the feet of the lepers and shared with them your water with noodles. You mortified your hide to the point of swooning. You enjoyed raptures, ecstasy, the gift of tears; you even got to hear voices, to see next to you a pillar of light that rose to the sky; you made light with a fistful of grass (you covered one breast and your sex with your hands); you forgot your senses and saw the emerald clarity, the serpent that appears before the chosen. The one you didn't see was Mortal, nor did you know what happened to him, nor did you remove his face from your chest, your only memory, sharper than thorns, looking at you, turning your guts inside out, buried in your heart like an amber.

So one day Mercy, who—rosary in hand—was dragging her feet over stones and bramble, thought she saw herself in the distance, advancing toward herself.

"Another miracle!"—she thanked the Giver aloud. She continued walking. Then she ran into Help.

"Let's sing!"—they exclaimed. (*And taking each other's hand*):

> There's neither scourge nor reward
> faithful the infidel
> The quick and the dead
> Dance with the Minstrel.

And they cried in their joy.

"I don't know how to say it"—sobbed One; and the Other:—"I don't know how to say it."

And so on till they calmed down, and untied their tongues. They were just turning the place into a lachrymatory with their tears when a bunch of drunken peasants came by. They sang as they walked, with canteens and sickles flung over their shoulders and a pickled stag on a pole. They laughed in a grand manner, so outrageous and insane did they find the weepers. They wanted to dance with them. They made signs with their hands touching themselves you know where, and in fun; they poked at one another. The girls seemed in such great need, with such appetites, that they threw them rolls and raisins. Although starving they tossed them back like hot coals and shouted that "the hunger they suffered was another kind; only the news of a Spaniard with skin like tasseled corn, a chaste tongue, and javelin eyes would satisfy them."

The men, laughing heartily:

"To Cadiz he goes, and on wings."

Hearing this made them so smiley and content that they asked for the same rolls and raisins they had just refused, not to mention meat, wine, and spices. Swiftly, they left.

They spent a happy day. By the next morning they were already confined in black cloth, one of them in a hairnet of starched cambric, the other with her bald disgrace still exposed. They took with them a mare, and lame at that, a missal and a jug of ginger. Had they killed a nun? Pillaged a convent? Where'd they get all those rags? I don't know.

Joy made them proliferate.

Already they play leapfrog and ring-around-the-rosy—"it is not weeping but the plucking of guitars that our Shepherd wants"—they lose the green ivy of their eyelids, they laugh, yes, just like the words say, they laugh and make haste, Mercy high on her saddle, under a fringed parasol which, opened, propels the animal when there's a good wind; Help in front, pulling the reins, parting the underbrush with her cane, crossing herself at every cliff.

MERCY: A day of merriment this is, since not of mourning. Let us not exhaust more hymnals since Mortal awaits us. He, before an absence split in two, is now a sole thirst drying us, a mute figure among stones.

HELP: Then we didn't know how to look for him. Ask for him. We felt his hunger and, crazy little feet, we ran all over the place.

MERCY: We were birds in air.

HELP: And now salamanders in fire!

Already the amazon unfolds parchments, wets her forefinger with saliva to feel the wind's direction, makes note of bird frequency, launches the filly to a gallop and hums "east" or "northeast," with her little flute voice.

When blown from the stern their contentment is great; they think Mortal is promoting their union and pushing them toward him.

MERCY (*first voice*)

> Look at me, and you will have eyes
> and I yours, to refresh my own.

And HELP (*second voice*):

> You entered me. You anointed my tonsure
> and like burning coals left my senses.

The duo frightened birds and lizards; snakes and bucks glided behind the black bramble to spy on them. The creaking wicker of their hampers held rugs, wooden saints and carbines; in a pot, among small laurel leaves, cumin, capers, and red pepper, a deer tail and two ears clanked. A good bullfight they must have put on to deserve such distinguished trophies!

So they searched, ay, but didn't find. Wounded with love they walked, ran through the fields. They smelled only of sweet basil and rosemary; they ate only grass and flowers; painted birdies, they crossed forests and streams in one thrust, they shouted at the top of their lungs to see if he heard them; they inscribed on their rings—tin hoops that were still theirs—the word WOUNDER, and they trained homing pigeons to carry them in all directions.

They paused at every tree, to see if he had engraved his name; they distinguished the different greens in the grass, searching for the faded trace of his soles; they spent their nights in silence, watching: they heard the sap push out the buds, the gills of fish palpitate, and faraway, on the other shore, the fire in the eyes of tigers, the sleep of men, the vigil of muezzins. A warm air enfolded them as if he had breathed it; then they dreamed intensely of him, to see if he'd appear, they repeated his name till they were breathless, to conjure it they wanted to invent him with words, count all fish, birds, and fruit, all vermin and bugs, to see if those that nourished him, that he crushed with his step, were missing.

They searched, ay, but didn't find. They wanted to give up, be someone else.

Pigeons under the moon, in great strides they crossed bridges, nights, valleys of white ruins. Finally they saw beyond the hills a light as if from many bright lamps, bounded by a strip of palms. It was the sea between lines of sand, a line of domes; between deltas of saltpeter, the blue dot of the fortified bay.

Comforted by the view of Cadiz, garland-clustered—guardian angels of the port—they praised and exalted as they laid a tablecloth down by a stream to thus recover their health and give thanks. They were relishing sunflowers with honey and gazing at ships cutting through terraces of foam, when they heard a sound like splitting rafts, and then some cries. Striped by the shadows of willows, fleeing mountain goats were approaching the bank. They jumped over the tablecloth. They turned over the pitcher of wine. After them came two naked, soaking shepherds. They stopped at the sight of wooden bowls, the toppled pitcher of red wine, the purple-stained grass, and frightened Help and Mercy, wounded partridges, open pomegranates in hand.

The Flamenco Girls stood up, and shyly turned their faces toward the stream. With one hand they covered their eyes—Help put a little mirror in front of hers to look at the shepherds without dishonoring herself—with the other, they pointed to the pitcher, accusingly.

The shepherds stammered "a good lunch to you," and with the wet underpants rumpled in their hands, they covered what they thought most urgent: the popular gesture of Modesty. Above the damp cloths their pubic hairs showed in minute spirals; other hairs, like down, shaded their chests. They were strong and golden and had identical beards and hair. The shepherds blushed at seeing them so covered: flowered cretonne fitted them snugly like shrouds from where their hands, desiccated herons, and shaven heads emerged; a white bow on their last lock crowned them like a weather vane. Under those consumptive butterflies the Deers smiled.

And offering the shepherds the bowl of pomegranates:

"Pray do not stop, your mountain goats are escaping."

"Yes, we were running after fleeing goats, and find ourselves before wounded fawns."

And that quaint music? It's hand organs. Look: turn the crank. Don't let the roll stop. That holey roll is the music. Time as a honeycombed parchment. I look at them. The Polliwogs enter Cadiz. The boys follow them in throngs, singing ballads and clapping. The organs of Cadiz slide their sounding boxes, painted with jumping turtles, silver flowers, and Indian birds, around Help and Mercy. And they escape, they don't want that music, they want Mortal's, which is silent music.[5]

They ask around for him. The saffron-haired players follow them, big puppets rolling cranks and heads. Hoods. And the girls cover their ears, hide in the doorways—are they crying? They want to give up, be someone else.

They searched, yes, they asked, they bribed, they begged for advice from door to door. Nobody understood them. People would push them. Throw them old bread and pots of rotten soup. They caught their fingers in doors.

---

5 In this passage, and many others, may Saint John forgive me.

Remained stuck there. Children threw stones at them. Cats came to sniff them.

_____ Fragments from Help and Mercy's Log Book

ONE

HELP: (*Isle and Islets of
the Queen.*[6]) Yes, I discern
this sea's roof is of fern,
and, its towers are lances.
Are they coral the lusters
on these insular clusters?
MERCY: No, they're holey countenances.
Don't you see that those red dots
are mushrooms and were eye slots
of turtles and drowned dancers?

_____ Fragment from Help and Mercy's Log Book

TWO

Yesterday the sea was orange-hued and calm. We saw a school of sirens come near the ship, some of them caught on to the prow and kept us company during many leagues.

6 An Archipelago south of Camagüey.

The sailors threw them walnuts and hazelnuts, which they like so much. It was joyous to see them frolic in the water.

Afraid of running over tritons at night, we navigated cautiously; these besieged us in bands of as many as one hundred and did not leave us till dawn, remaining tangled in gulfweed. Many birds and angels, never further than a mile away from the coast, flew by; land must be near…"We saw a branch of fire fall into the sea."[7]

This morning, fish, green bands in the water—islands? Help danced for the sailors, clad only in sea shell necklaces…I said a Salve Regina.

A wind blows from the stern and sea horses stick to the hull. Help caught some and fried them in oil. The sailors, it seems, found them delicious. A long siesta. We're running out of drinking water.

SUBSEQUENT REPORTS identify Help and Mercy as two organists in the cathedral of Santiago, Cuba. The Bacardí Museum holds in its collection of engravings two scores that they composed and, in all probability, in their own handwriting: one is a Stabat Mater. If rather simple in instrumentation, the text is correct. The other is a vernacular song about love and Cupid's artful deceptions, followed by a quadrille for clavichord; both are undated in the original. Which is the composer of each work, and if a "Mourning Song" in two voices, for soprano and contralto, also belongs to the composer of the first, and if "To the pineapple and sun of Cuba," a song for mezzosoprano and pi-

7 Columbus.

ano, clearly sweetened by the Italian operetta, belongs to the composer of the second, are debatable matters, but after all, secondary.

Other news less worthy of credit—handed down by dubious oral tradition—testifies that the famous women who, following the route of the liberating invasion, entertained the island in sheds, or under white pilgrim and nomadic tents, are none other than the Moorish Girls.

Engravings of the times, anonymous or signed by local craftsmen, portray the *Ontos* Girls against a background of banners and tapers.

But if these episodes are but rough drafts, written over them have remained those that took place during the last days of Cadiz and the first of Santiago. There's a log book in which the Fixed Eyes bear witness to the exaltation which "the incandescence of the tropics" produced in them and they even indulge in a dialogued ten-line stanza, silly and metrically precise, on the Isles and Islets of the Queen, an archipelago off the southern coast of Camagüey.

It is after the landing that their common history branches off, or duplicates itself in mocking inversion, as if the facts danced dizzily around themselves.

We shall follow the version that covers the days of choral glory in the Santiago cathedral, up until the disappearance of the organists in Havana, victims of a snowstorm.

DOMUS AUXILII

1: Hey, by the way, what happened to Mortal? Don't they keep searching for him, have they forgotten him?

"Why honey!"—Help answers, and cartwheels out of her hammock. "Have some, kid, it'll cool you off"—and she gives me a guanábana milk shake.

I (*delicious!*) tip the glass: Through the bottom I see her
    within a milky circle, sugar-stained and concave.

"What can I do for you, sweetie?"—she continues. (*How she's changed! I say to myself.*) "Reality is a simple matter of birth and death, so why worry ourselves sick? If you don't change, you get stuck, pal, so live and let live!"

I put the glass down to hear her better. She waves her hands, shuffles around, talks with her hands on her hips.

"Look, honey, we searched for him all right, but if he turns up, great, and if not (*she yawns, ooh, it looks like she's going to swallow me*) we'll get through the day with the help of siesta. Which of the two is blonder?" (*And she raises—what sunlight!—a bamboo curtain.*)

Pale sunflowers speckle her body: reflections from a stained-glass window. Shadows of arabesques break between her hands: iron grates, city blocks of pink glass. The light scratches her, a smell of molasses surrounds her, the purple of the roofs hardly differs from that of her eyes.

I: I've got to admit, Help, you're really at home here. The
    gold of these tropical fruits glows no brighter than
    the gold of your hair, angels of Caney county crown
    you with medlars, write your name on mameys.

HELP: Come on, sonny, don't be so Cuban. (*and calling*)
    Mercy, Mercy, listen to what this aborigine (*that's me*)
    is saying.

MERCY: In some mood for natives I am!—She comes in from the kitchen, half-naked, with a bunch of bananas hanging from her waist and singing:

> Mamá those singers so gay
> are they from ol' Havana bay?
> oh how I like their rhythm
> oh how I'd like to know them...

She flops in a wicker chair. And fans herself with a palm leaf, opening her legs in a way that to tell the truth leaves me perplexed. It's incredible how heat loosens folks up. But let's cut this short and move on to something else.

Let's climb to the lecterns of the Schola Cantorum. Before them the Passion Flowers have been decaying, extravagant vestry junk, holy water larvae. Poor things, they spend the night among these platforms, ringing the bells and oiling the organs. Their days go by in Te Deums, siestas, and bread with sardines. When they leave the cathedral, pious mustached women shout at them from behind curtains, envious of the clerical life they lead, organizing catechism and bingo parties (they nickname them The Bats). Sunday afternoons, services over, they slip away to dance at the Medlar, so they say. There they rub against mulattos and slanty-eyed natives; they go drunk to the beer halls, to wait for morning—remembering Mortal?—in the bacchanal.

That winds them up for another week of climbing the

tower. But, as they say, you can't ring the bell and march in the procession, and this gig of the Little Shopping Bags is in for a bad ending.

When did the Mulatto first come before them? How did his diplomaed tenor voice, his violin, fill that vociferous old age with enthusiasm? How did he gain access, not to chapels and vestry, but to tower platforms, and to the most secret beds? He made the organs resound and, long live the virgin!, the Cranachian bellies of their organists.

HELP: He brought those yellowing texts back to life with his sweet breath!

MERCY: He scared away the moths with his nigger smell!

These devout women were already moving from the Spanish ascesis to Creole mysticism; they were the martyrs and confessors of half of Santiago (virgins they were not), but they bore one dead weight: their scales. So, seeing them pedal in vain, and finger sixteenth notes instead of thirty-seconds, and scribbles instead of eighth notes, the Bishop of the diocese, that plump good-natured fellow with clammy hands, ordered that an "expert" assist them, since "it takes more than fervor to play the organ" and "my daughters, technique is everything in divine matters." Yes, the canon was a technocrat, so the next day, come what may, he unswervingly appeared in the deambulatory arm in arm with the violinist. The latter came in a Bachian jacket, with his kinky hair slicked down; when he took up the bow, his hands fluttered like two long-tailed doves. He was merry and frolicsome, and from the minute he saw Help and Mercy he knew that high music was in store for them.

"If in the towers"—said the sepia Paganini, taking from his sleeves a lace handkerchief—"there were spiral ramps for carriages, we could set up the clavichords and, chorus raised, sing a Salve Regina that would be heard out to sea!"—And he drew in the air with his handkerchief, the form of a pineapple.

"Oh!"—breathed Help, braking with the pedal.

"Let's sing!"—ordered Bruno. And he gave the key.

Oh the sadness, my friend, of those middays! Of cockroach skies, yellow rain. Big birds would hover among the ropes of the bell tower or fall shrieking, beheaded against the lightning rod. But neither the little heads throbbing between the cracks of the boarded floor, nor the blood-clotted feathers prevented Help and Mercy from attacking the midday onion pie. They'd eat it standing, among bunches of Easter ribbons, remains of ramsacked sepulchers, and moldings from the kneeling stool.

They would cry from two to four, rolled into balls among the cushions of a confessional. They would cry and sneeze, and it was neither snuff nor something similar that they smelled, but rather the fine dust of the covers, sand that saturated the naves, suspending—golden asterisks—fleas and lice.

Figure it out: two hours daily of lachrymal secretion, with the little they'd drink and the lot they'd urinate—thus the prosperity of the east gardens: gargoyles emptied into them—and you'll see why they were drying up, like pickled lizards.

Around four, that old devil siesta would start putting the flea in their ear. To shake it out they'd ring bells and vespers a few times, drink some cane liquor (which they'd send up in a thermos bottle in the morning, along with other victuals) and they'd give their all to the rigors of the ruled staff. On the bells, fleeing the clappers, blind baby owls would bump their heads.

To judge by the concentric iridescent veins (so pretty!) which daily tears left in the felt of the cushions, the weeping season was long and full. You can see that they resisted—did the memory of Mortal still sustain them?—the sudden attacks of the honeyed heat; you can see that disorder frightened them.

Till one day: (1) They grew little ovoid bellies which waddled before them as they'd climb the spiral staircase; (2) they got bored with everything, they shat on scales and theory, they let their hairs split and dirt settle on the suspenders of their slips; (3) to everything they answered "whatever you say, pal" "no need to kill yourself." In short: siesta corroded their bones, turned them yellow, a malignant anemia; no big deal, it just gave them the Caribbean torpor (sweetly!) in its mildest form, which is the cabbage soup, and the daily *danzón,* and the mattress.

They'd remain stupified on the platforms for days on end, never descending to the maddening crowd, only opening tin cans and playing cards. So that at noon one day, the priest, accompanied by the plump theocrat, climbed the creaking steps on all fours and surprised them, at Te Deum hour, in full snore.

"Better tuned"—exclaimed the servant of the servants of the lord—"are your fluty bronchial tubes, than those of this dilapidated harmonium!"

And in their drowsiness, talking through their noses,

they flapped their hands in his face. "Come on pal, we're up to our necks in pedaling. We finger the keyboard all day long and not a single saint comes down. We entreat in vain. There's a great deafness up there. We've had it: our phalanx, second phalanx, and third phalanx hurt from fingering that keyboard so much!"

Now that you've heard them, darlings, you'll understand why when Bruno, jazzy violinist and steady drinker of Santiago *prú,* arrived, he found the way paved.

This will look redundant, but the classes began in perfect harmony. The virtuoso taught them Misereres, but also sarabands, so from the Salve Regina, alas, they soon went on to the chaconne. How did he introduce them to the daiquiri, the baroque crown of Oriente province drinks? How did they become so addicted to the Santiago *"chiringuito"*? Where did they learn the *"saoco"* recipe, that is: *agua-ardiente* with cocoanut milk, which they were already pronouncing like Cubans as *"agüecoco"*? Who taught them that bad habit: leaving tamales, pork pies, and deviled ham rolls among the organ strings, where they'd sometimes even rot?

Already the cover of the organ, shining more from varnish than from centenaries, was a washboard marked with whitish circles: the traces of small glasses of crushed ice, overflowing with Bacardí and maraschino cherries, which they left there, in the frantic dancing. And I say frantic dancing, because while One scribbled four or five *pasodobles* on the artefact, the Other danced off heat in the arms of the Maestro, when he wasn't in those of Rita Pla, the new pupil, an image seller and a soprano in her free time.

When they had celebrated the dancing gods, they'd go back to the lessons. How nice those trios were, with Bruno in the center of the organ and the Blond Cowlicks on either side, industriously following his hands with theirs, from C to C, from keyboard to knee, yes sir, they'd give him a finger and he'd take the rest! Do you remember Help, your hair messed by the blowing tubes, coiling your matted peroxide hair around them, golden serpents on golden pillars, musical taffy that you were, you naughty wench?

HELP (*a bit grief-stricken*): Yes, kid, of course I remember; how can I forget those times? Listen, get me a drink…What could have become of those waterfront bars, the Black and White, the Two Worlds, where we'd end up shipwrecked in the morning? What became of the Santiago by-the-hour hotels, those gardens open only for the few? Mercy would run naked among colonists and Haitian smugglers, dancing Lully's dances, as she would call those drum beatings…

(*And we hear a Lully dance which becomes a* voodoo *drumbeat. We go back to the times of the cathedral tower.*)

AT THE SANTIAGO MUSEUM

neither detailed branches, earthly paradises, faces made of vegetables, nor patient gardens painted leaf by leaf were scarce.

Peeping out of the windows of their Noah's Arks, their

manes in flames, varnished little blond giraffes passed by. Restorers had returned the eloquence of cockatoos and the gold of roosters to the palms. On the same branches hummingbirds and mockingbirds perched. Among the stones, white and quartered like the giraffes, lizards slept; the one with little vertical ears, the rodent, would flit through the reeds—the raw red of its scalped hide denounced it—.

In the engravings Latin alternated with old French in humpbacked letters.

"Ara chloroptere! Boselphus Trago Canelus!"—Mercy would exclaim pointing to the little spheres of fish scales bristled with thorns: miniatures of haddock and snappers.

And the hummingbird sewn to the wood, pinned flyer.

In the Other Room

"Place of Arms on The Night of the Military Parade" and a blurred "View of Havana," by Hill, were gathering dust. Sugary Indians displayed tobacco leaves and cassava pies. Then the collection, the Punishment of the Mace, Punishment of the Mask, and Punishment of the Stocks: Negroes tainted in blood, kneeling among shackles and chains.

Christ Sets Out from Santiago

Along the naves, tapers in little cups of glided edges were

blinking; in the dark those signs were bat eyes nailed against the altars or swarms of glowworms coming out of a bottle. That light of drizzled sand over Help and Mercy would change them at times into water nymphs, and other times into little candy skulls, depending on how the shadows cut them.

The murmur of crackling wax would join the sound of a rusty clock and this the steps of their bare feet. The feet of the Devout Ones scarcely touched the floor, like a hanged man's feet. Beneath the gravestones they were stepping on, among mushrooms and withered relics, lay eight mitered generations: empty eyes would look at the same archivolts, the identical days would from the lantern yellow the circles of angels in the dome, as light as mist; bundles of bones held in place the gold of the tunics that were encrusted in them, and pressed together, dried cartilage, reliquaries and chalices.

Heads bowed, Help and Mercy advanced toward the vestry. They went reading the In Memoriam engraved in the marble. They touched dark green texts with the tip of their forefingers and crossed themselves. They heard a warbling: it was Rita Pla's vocal exercises. When they pushed open the doors, they found her before Bruno who was raising a baton, her mouth open like someone who's about to spell in the first reading book Acorn Air And.

There was a lukewarm air, of wax, among the closets, and a mustard light among the holy-water pots, incensories and purple puppets with their eyelids on backward. Light filtered through a yellow awning, stretched before the baroque iron work of the window; the wind stretched it—a drum—blowing it—a sail—. Birds were crossing lines on the cloth, and the trolleycars with their long sparking trolleys, in the background of the orange square, outlined by the iron bars, were gods of codices running with burning rattles.

Mercy opened the little platinum mesh pouch that she wore at her waist and out of it came a swollen key, with a double point. She carefully sank it into the lock. The click rang like a bell.

Sprawled in a corner of the display case, elbows folded against his chest and his arm in disks, the Redeemer, foot and headless, was resting. Hooks came out of his wrists and ankles, and from his neck, cut at the Adam's apple, a great screw. He had neither sex nor knee. A tortoise-shell varnish covered him and on his stomach, pale pink. He was worm-eaten. He smelled of incense and naphthalene. On the wounded side you could see a hinge.

On a slab of white wood, stained with ink from the sign HANDLE WITH CARE, his feet and a hand of ovaled nails were exhibited. The other, which gripped a golden flagstaff, and the head, were found in the back of a drawer among broken candelabrums, little Santa Lucía eyes and scapularies.

They put him together in the twinkling of an eye. Bruno screwed on his head until the two little threads of blood which ran down from his eyes continued into those of his neck. Rita combed his beard and with a beer-drenched curler twisted his wig of blond hemp into several snail shell curls which she fastened with a barbed-wire crown. Help perfumed him with her "Attractive and Winning." She took out her string of safety pins. They dressed him in a ruffled slip, crackling with starch and on top, a blanket of rubies and stones from El Cobre Mountain, and snail shells on a string. In his bullfighter's garb he balanced on his flat feet, in the middle of the vestry.

The Christ Fans stepped back to look at him. When they came forward again, they fell on their knees.

WITH GREEN BACKGROUND AND SHOUTING _____

"Praised be Jesus Christ our Lord who died on the cross to redeem us!"—Help shouted praises till she was hoarse, stretching the e's of "redeem" to the point of choking, catching the impulse in soprano and, poor wretch, ending in bass.

"Have pity on us, ay!" (That was Mercy, and she struck her chest as if she were seized with Saint Vitus's Dance.)

"Long live the King of the Jews and the Cubans!" (That was Rita and she sobbed with emotion.)

And He, before Bruno, looked at Himself in the mirror.

"Look how handsome, look how handsome He is!"—shouted a little black girl hanging from the bars of the window.

On the street, cars with loudspeakers passed by; the nasal twang of amplifiers came in along with the crackling of broken glass and screeching of rails.

In the tarnished space of the mirror the small doors opened and the red square of the bonnet, the lace sleeve, the black shirt frills of lively golds appeared: it was the Bishop.

"Oh, my beloved!"—and he patted his stomach.

Through the crack between the shutters you could see

a shining in the naves: the dirty silver of the altars, reddish disks dancing clumsily—copper crosses—.

In the damp vestry the faithful were five hanged warriors, going around and around in the same place, dervishes, spinning tops, merry-go-rounds. The grass green, bottle green floor of rhombi met the orange walls at sharp angles, forming a cuneiform space where he reigned, duplicated in the river of quicksilver.

"Hurry up, girls, we'll be leaving in a minute!"—And the Lord Bishop shook a hand bell that was heard again, faraway, returning from the dome.

And he shook a hand bell that was heard again, another time, as if it had sounded in the Kingdom of Death.

"We're leaving!"—In the naves a band of cracked drums, water-filled guitars, and muted rattles broke out.

What a hissing of prayers! What a creaking of benches! Chest beatings. Ejaculations. The weepers sounded maracas—they played maracas for this burial—and the hoodmasters their mahogany clavichords. Little devils with palm-leaf skirts and castles of yellow feathers on their heads crowded into the baptistery.

He appeared in the door of the vestry, tottering under a canopy of royal palms held up by Help and Mercy, within a white white light, as from milk curds. Canticles and cheers. Under His vault of greenery He advanced among purple strips of stained-glass windows, shadows of banners, flags.

The sepulcher awaited Him.

You could hear a flapping of wings, like droves of geese: it was the Black Oblates, dressed as angels.

These big Pious Babies were already lined up in the

choir aisle, rosy and smelling of Eau de Cologne, in white pique dresses and carrying large palm-leaf baskets, reciting a rosary of river pebbles and sweating into initialed hankies.

Grumpy dwarfs were stamping their feet behind the altar, wrapped in bunches of red felt ribbon.

The shrouds were replicas of His face, the standard-bearers' ensigns the color of His blood, the cornet of the Municipal Brass Band the silver of His tomb.

"Long live the King of Alto Songo!"—that was the hot-headed misses of the diocese, who had been tippling as they walked since morning. One of them rattled a maraca.

Electric tapers were lit. Crepe-paper flowers carpeted the roll to the sepulcher. Make way, people, here comes the Verb of Santiago! The resurrected, sandpapered King was about to begin the voyage on His aluminum throne. The blood barely stained His nose and eyelids. Why it looked like He was going to laugh!

Now the leader shakes his baton (at his age, that's what he shakes best). And the chorus sings the first Gloria— What a triumph for Bruno! Mercy leaves the pulpy palm leaves on the pulpit staircase. She kisses Him, sets Him on the sepulcher.

Help shouts "Ready!" Someone breaks into tears.

The King totters, then takes off, balancing under a rain-fall of jasmine. He advances toward the portico, between lamps of green glass. The flame flits over the chalk of His face, the shine of rotten fish. White and green, the rust of nails, flowers of tetanus, opens in His dried hands and pierced feet.

"Here comes the handsomest fellow of Caney county"—the children clap hands. And take out their bags of confetti.

Creole gentlemen follow Him. You've got to admit, that humble vestry wine sure gives a man poise! They march in unison, foot to foot, their stomachs tucked in by In Excelsis Deo sashes.

The Minstrels march, the precious load on their shoulders: in front, Mercy sets the example in her Prussian blue rayon cloak with a cushion sewn on the left shoulder, and Rita Pla, a cushion on her right shoulder, struts in such a way that you'd think it's the lantern of The Bakers' Masked Ball that's being carried and not the Victor of Santiago on His tomb. The poor Redeemer up there, He must be eating Himself up! At the rear, Help, in the best of her wigs, and Bruno hold the two back handles of the sepulcher. Look in wonder, brethren, at what four pillars carry the Blond of Blonds, at what caryatids fit for a mausoleum, in short, what four legs for a bench!

Already they're down the central nave. At His passing the faithful close their eyes, kneel; trembling, they kiss the carpet where He has passed. And make the sign of the cross. Others run. Push. Touch Him. Tear white lilies from His funeral carriage.

Already they're near the portico. From the high altar you can see Him from the back, outlined against the blue rectangle of night, shower of light; hands and handkerchiefs raised. The stones from El Cobre shrine, mortuary jewels, are already glittering on His cloak, stirred by the breeze in the square.

"Lower Him!"—Mercy orders—"or His crown will short-circuit on the bulbs of the tympan!"

The bearers stoop. He's outside. The whole square lights up.

"Raise Him again!"

And He ascends, standing erect over the sepulcher, proud as a pimp, hoisting a white flag. Behind, red stones, gold stains: the seal of His face on the Pantocrator of Italian mosaic. A silence. Rosary beads passing through fingers. Candles crackling.

The wind on the terraces, whistling through patio palm trees.

Then bells, the hymn. Gentlemen in drill suits and Panamas come out on their balconies, and little girls in straw hats empty baskets of petals. Cigar smoke sweetens the air in slow rings that will break among the fans. The square is full. The people of Santiago sing.

"Straight on, but *moderato,* gents, *per piacere!*"—orders Bruno. And the Blond descends the steps, following a gentle parabola as if on an escalator. The Bishop receives Him.

No sooner did He set foot on the ground when beneath the portico appears the sorrowful, ash moon Virgin. They've whitened her with rice powder, "so that she truly looks pale," her mouth and cheeks, a heart. Her tears, and her seven daggers, are silver.

He crosses the square. Around Him trumpets, the rim of the drums, crashing cymbals, shine. The Bishop makes way for Him; covered in his hands, the chalice: over the

red cloth of his sleeves, gilded lace. In front walk two acolytes swaying incensories. Sinuous ribbons of white smoke.
The pale parson mumbles Latin mumbo jumbo as he goes,
and makes crosses in the air with his right hand. Women
in black mantillas and high shell combs, and stiff men with
candles and branches of lilies, walk on either side.

"Come, people of Santiago, who's more stud than He,
and who whiter? "—howl the Cornucopias of Craniums,
beating their breasts.

HELP (*who has pinched a cloak with a black and white fiber
hood.*): You leave Santiago to enter Death!

MERCY (*wielding a shroud in which you see Christ's face in an
arrow pierced heart with the inscription "C loves M."—
Christ and Mercy*): You enter Death to give us Life!

The old people, bundled up, crowd together on the
sidewalks, beneath the greenish halo of the street lamps.
Joining hands they watch Him go by in His Sunday best,
and then withdraw in silence, to kneel on the cushions of
the antechamber.

In cracked oil paintings the Virgin shines on her half-
moon, against a blackened sky of sugar mill chimneys,
and in the yellowish cardboard of screens a mulatto Christ
watches over Santiago: a labyrinth of small sugar planta-
tions and boats.

> Look at them oh crack footed King,
> because you leave they cannot sing

It's Rita, when they stop in front of City Hall where
gentlemen greet Him from the gates, waving hats. Little
devils jingle bells, dancing on one foot before the sepul-

cher. Against the white façades, the hood masters play their clavichords: black stitches around the holes of their eyes.

Then the procession moves on. Empty terraces, lighted lamps, wicker rocking chairs rocking are left behind, and in the shadows of interiors: burnished clocks, mirrors, opulent pineapple goblets, the ancestral portrait.

In the night's dampness they disappear into poplar groves, into the suburbs.

Now, little by little, they are left alone. In the city the tapers' light has traced a white sign, a chalk omega, two inverted fish joined by a thread. Or perhaps a signature.

So they left the last lots behind, the whistle of the land breeze through the mangrove trees, the streaks of saltpeter on the eaves. When they started moving into the thick night, Bruno made Him turn His head so that He'd see the rows of windows slowly disappear. Mercy tells that down His cheeks rolled two big tears, and also down His neck, as far as His shoulder blade.

When they straightened His head He saw before Him other greens, the surprise of other birds in the calm, the Cuban peasants: little eyes behind windows, lighter than the royal palm leaves of the shutters, Chinese shadows—but in big Panama hats—in front of carbon lamps. They covered the cracks in their walls with newspapers, passed the latch, and between the planks of their whitewashed doors, they peeped out to see Him go by. The huts were boxes of hemp, the cracks small yellow stained-glass windows with printed letters.

They followed the windings of a stream, the highway, they disappeared into the mist of a small forest, among the dark cones of the…(and here, the exhaustive enumeration of Cuban trees—horseflesh mahogany, guamá, jequi, oak, the anona tree, and so forth—with their botanical jargon)[8]…until Help and Mercy, Rita and Bruno, "dead tired," left the sepulcher on the grass.

In the early morning—or was it the turning of a rattle-snake among dry leaves, the flapping of an owl?—they heard Him cough. He woke up with stiff elbows and wrists; the joints of His ankles rigid. Well you see, it's just that accustomed as He was to vestry climate, tempered by the sighs and yawns of so many fasters, the dampness had gotten into the sawdust of His bones. His fingers stiffened, one foot hard in the air as if on a step, He was petrified in a good-bye: poorly sewn puppet, raffle picture card. His meeting with the Cuban countryside, with insular space and its glowworms, had brought on arthritis.

They stretched His limbs as much as they could. They put Him through calisthenics, recited an Ex Aegypto Israel. The heat was—listen to Help—"thicker than pea soup." There was something sweetish in the air, as if near a beehive or cane juice stand.

The followers stretched—the few that were left: at the sight of the jungle the rest had resigned themselves to urban mysticism—shook the hay off their uniforms and cassocks and ran into the woods to piss.

8   Phonetic delights never omitted in any Cuban tract, from the *Mirror of Patience*—1608—to the present day.

(Tarnished cornets, and on the drums, dew.)

He felt that something was jolting Him in the knees, that His legs were giving way. A shiver ("Oh Father, have pity on me, you who have gotten me into this mess"—He thought). His whole body itched—Was it jigger fleas? He promised to scourge Himself. He wasn't going to wait much longer. Listen to these morning prayers:

HELP (*who was putting the pink back into her cheeks with rouge*): Now you carry Him for a while, why it's worse than carrying a chimpanzee piggyback. He's got me crippled.

MERCY (*who was bathing in a stream*): You poke your own hellfire, you lazybones, ramrod, thick clod. Etc., etc.

Stretching and bending they finally reached a town. What a relief for their swollen feet: the square was paved in cobblestones and dark green water ran along the juncture of the stones. It overflowed from the broken basin of the fountain.

What a smell of coffee, what nice smoke spiraling out the doorways! Bowls of chipped china on shiny crimson tablecloths, the leaning tables, the stools, piled on top.

The women were doing the foot scratching dance, coming out in flowered slippers, the backs of them worn down: "oh boy, what a visitor." They opened their houses. Brought out lamps and hung them on the *guásima* trees in the patio, and gave away lumps of pan sugar from their cupboards. Why they combed their hair: to receive Him!

The Next Day

An arcade stood facing the village, and another one almost parallel: the shadow of the first on the smooth, windowless façades. These successive arches supported unfinished walls, or ruins, a second portico, and the slope of roofs. On a stoop rested the handle of a coach, and over the shadow of its great wheels, on the adjacent wall, hung carbines, telescopes, pendulums, and perhaps pocket pistols and swords with tortoise-shell hilts. From there the early risers set forth in a throng, with great clamor and large red shawls around their necks. They brought accordions. Graters and maracas. What cute music they scratched! It would split anybody's sides! It was a thick-lipped mulatto with even, scorched kinky hair—Mercy's darling—who was shooting off like this, with his razor sharp voice:

> I have a little thing that you like
> that you like
> that you like

He wriggled like an eel, with a hand on his hip—what Dahoman rings!—pointing with the other to the object of such elliptic verse.

The aroma of honest-to-good coffee—accustomed as He was to that of incense—and that spicy odor emanating from the tables revived Him. He was delighted that they ran behind Him, that they wore down the wood of His feet with kisses, that they perfumed Him with *agua-ardiente*. He wanted them to entreat Him, but with guitars and gourds; He wanted angels with royal palms. He thought Himself a patriot, a Marti-like orator frozen in the threads of an engraving; He pictured Himself in a speech-making pose, raised to a tricolor tribune, or releasing a fighting cock with His calloused hands, its feathers crossing His dried, olive face. He would like you to see a blue sky behind Him, and a sun of hard fog, a waning moon, several comets. He had the calling of a redeemer, Blondie did, He liked flags.

Help immediately joined in on the fun not to mention— which would be knocking your head against Redundance —Rita and Bruno, who didn't have to join it, since they had it in them since birth (according to Mercy).

It wasn't till they were in the store, with the "hurry up, we still have the fringes to put up," that they found out: the one they left slipping on the cobblestones outside in the square was not the object of this great fuss; the people were expecting a new candidate, who had promised "to give the town running water and to build a road that would connect them to their neighbors in nearby towns," to arrive at noon. For him the tournament, the cockfights, the "National" band, the tables of breadsticks and the taffy wrapped in colored papers.

Competition horses in checkered girths came from all over the county. And on foot, pulling their reins, smiling bowlegged riders already appeared in black and gold or blue and gold colors that reappeared on stirrups and blinders, bringing Guinea hens and Mandarin oranges and shopping bags of limes too.

"May you be struck down by lightning!"—Mercy exploded, she was cracking up, already wallowing in corners with some of the band players (according to Help), knocking machetes and spats off the walls.

"God, what am I doing here?"—and she ran toward the portico through the steam of boiled milk, the wake of clean pitchers and the marimbas.

She sensed that the party was leaving her. She saw Bruno call to her, between two open-mouthed guitarists, against a background of pots and swords.

In full force she crossed the square, fell on her knees before Christ and cried on His navel—that's as high as her disheveled head could reach.

"Forgive me Dear God, I didn't know what I was doing." (*and without any sense of dramatic transition*) Help adds: "Fungus! Pustules on his feet! He's rotting, eek!"

She took one step back, and another, without turning around. She opened her hands, drew them near her eyes, scrutinized the palms:

"And I've touched Him! I'm infected: alcohol!"

And He, to get a good look at her, squeezed His glass pupils, those opaque stones that have been dimmed by so much looking at the top of a locker. He was soaked with dew. Bagasse Christ. One foot was eczematous and green, and in the arch a milky flower, of mushrooms. His nose ran and so did the swollen edge of His eyelids.

"Alcohol, for God's sake!"—And she shot off to the store.

"And the best!"—answered Bruno who awaited her with open arms in the doorway. And he emptied on her head a glass of rum-on-the rocks. From there He was dragged away. Help and Mercy, yoked together, pulled

Him. He went on foot, tied to a beam, handcuffed. They had taken off His crown and put on a palm-leaf hat because it was drizzling; they had tossed lemon juice on His foot and cologne on His head. So that His sore couldn't be seen, they had surrounded Him with vases of wax flowers. So that the Rotten One emerged from an opaque garden whose leaves the cart's jolting could not shake off. They fell into gutters. Got stuck in bogs.

Mercy was getting eaten up by mosquitoes; but stoically she sang:

> tonight it is raining
> tomorrow will be muddy,

When Help answered her the rain fell thicker:

> poor is the carter
> who pulls this cart

And the Foul One went through the drizzle, His feet among flowered urns, His legs among still flowers. Oh how it burns! Water surrounded Him right up to His pustules.

"A bigamist I'll be, but not a fag"—He thought. And looked out the corner of His eye at Bruno, who was laughing, envious.

It was because the Two Women were rubbing Him with camphor balls, wrapping Him in blankets, inserting in each armpit "because you see, He had fever on only one side" a vulvous thermometer with filigrees and Roman numerals. They even pleaded with Saint Lazarus to rid Him of galloping leprosy.

They had to cross the rising Jobabo river, and hauled the cart by looping the rope through a ring that moved along a rope tied to a palm tree on each bank. And the last just men kept the balance.

Like a rolling barrel full of stones was the noise of the waters. Red turtles leapt to the beams, held on with their little nails, disappeared into slow eddies. Trout jumped up in rapid flight, flicked their tails, spattered water, and remained gasping between planks.

"They fish themselves, God's creatures! Let's pray He doesn't decide to multiply them now!" (Help)

Below, the current dragged away torn roots, and shrubs with nests.

"And the bluish hands of drowned men, saying good-bye!" (Adds Mercy, who scarcely breathes so as not to move, "not everybody walks on water.") They left the rest of the pilgrimage in Oriente province waving handker-chiefs and sneezing. Rita wanted to catch on to the rope and swim to the other side, but they finally convinced her to stay on land. Bruno left the violin cover and three can-delabrums with her, to lighten the load. What a farewell! They could still see her from the other bank, behind the strip of mud, moving the three bronzes like a traffic cop. Then she became a blur with the others. At the landing a gust of wind carried away His hat. Bruno raised Him by the head and planted Him on the grass. Then they saw those plaques of pus which whitened His leg to the waist.

They stuck their ears to His stomach, the Magdalenas auscultated Him. Something was bubbling inside.

MERCY (*her eyes popping*): "The Evil Disease!"

The sweet felt of their earlobes and the pearls of their earrings rubbing His groin certainly seemed to make Him mighty happy. What a pity there wasn't a camera at hand: He was smiling!

ILLUSTRIOUS SHORES, but a feeble welcome did He receive from those of Santa María del Puerto del Príncipe.

Listen to those welcomes the Camagüeyan ladies forced on Him, sheltered behind the shutters and rails of their windows:

a. You will leave our towers mute, but the bronze of our many bells will sink your ships. (*They had taken Him for a pirate!*)

b. Ill wind from a leprosarium, angel of rebels, leader of escaped slave.

c. Locust of cattle, salting of the water, etc.

He, who in so many Gobelins, on so many night tables: wounded pigeon, gentleman of painted plaster, with eyes of chemical blue like a Mexican doll, He, whose signs—parallel fish, crowns, crosses and nails—embellished the glass of every paperweight and, in cement, worn down by rains, the medallions of every façade,

He, who appeared in so many family portraits.

And yet they did not recognize Him.

He scratched what He thought most symbolic of the situation (He already had Cuban habits!) and gave Bruno the "forward march" signal.

The shadows of dates clouded His face, in the black gardens of las Mercedes, the chandelier of the choir loft's arches. He wanted to lose Himself in the labyrinths of the angel makers, among the goldsmith stands and old book stalls. Along the banks of the Tínima River the display cases of Spanish flea markets, beyond the yellow halo of candles, were shining in the mist: Catalan panels with beheaded saints and all the arteries of their necks; paintings of balloons rising with sacks of sand and green ribbons: in the baskets, in smoking jackets, handlebar mustaches, and spectacles, brave Matías Perezes would observe the clouds.

BRUNO'S STATEMENT

It is here necessary to make note of a fact, so that written evidence shall remain which could serve the authoress in securing either total absolution or perpetual hellfire. Here it is: the Redeemer pointed to one of those balloons. It is well known that ascensions are His weak point.

I bear witness that, with the few pesos she had left, with no hope whatsoever of earning more, and much less in such chaste places, Help offered to get it for Him, perhaps because she had seen new stains on Him and knew that sooner or later she'd recover the gift. Whatever the case may be, she went out to buy it.

Every Venetian blind fell. Every salesman spat on her, threw the door in her face.

The lights went out. I hereby testify that that's how the Camagüeyan tour ended.

They saw black propellers among the palm trees: army helicopters were following them. Clean shaven young pilots descended to the villages He was going to pass through, to intimidate the people and buy Paloma de Castilla crackers. When the travelers arrived, little men in uniforms would point to them with large pencils and, terrified, take off. Through the plastic bellies of the crafts you could see them gesticulate and open maps.

To bother Him, the pilots powdered Him from above with bread crumbs.

Another rumble. They all stooped down—except Him, naturally, He would have hurt His pustules—but they didn't see anything. It was the subway.

There is no rule without the exception: the herbalists of Ciego de Avila came out to receive Him, and with a lot of noise. To entertain Him they brought out wooden serpents coiled around little mirrors, mortars, old pomander boxes with the names of leaves where letters were missing, the covers adorned with Florentine and French landscapes.

Mechanical gargoyles followed them, raising whirlwinds with their helices, five bakelite birds. Curtains of dust surrounded Him. If the three faithfuls would stop, the noise of the motors would decrease and the row of transparent machines would stand still in air, perpendicular to the highway. The whirlwinds would then spread and a spiral of straw would surround them.

If they'd flee to the grottos of reinforced concrete, or hide by the rivers, in the inns on abandoned piles, the patrol—and the dull buzzing—would escort them, forming a V whose vortex, a craft with two propellers, would plane over His head, like a Holy Spirit Dove.

HELP (*and the motors came on louder*):......(she opened and
   closed her mouth—was she shouting?—; gusts of
   wind stiffened her face. A totally bald pate.)

MERCY:......(*With calm gestures*)

Bruno touched them and pointed to the mouth of a
subway. They went down the escalator, under the panel
SUBWAY. With Him and the cart on their backs they passed
through a lunch counter (ay, His toes were already spout-
ing pus, falling off in pieces), the cabarets of River Side
(pustules had begun on His other leg and, like a belt of
rotting metals, they girded His stomach), corridors with
amplifiers; on the radio the twelve o'clock noon gongs,
the meowing sopranos on the Chinese programs and the
Candado soap commercials.

They bathed Him in sulphur. They came up in the elevator content, out the other mouth of the subway. Motionless, like a band of scabby turkey buzzards, the helicopters were waiting for them at the exit.

The din of the choppers were breaking Help's eardrums; the corruption of the Corpus Christi, Mercy's
heart.

The crafts were not following them at equal distances
now, but rather, one by one, they dove down like
kingfishers, almost flush with roofs and trees; then a hatch-
door opened in the plexiglass shell, the copilot peered out
a second "like the cuckoo of a clock" (Bruno), and took a
flash photograph. The mosquito would then return to
his place in the V. The next would come down.

Having reached the cherry orchards of Las Villas, He asked
them to abandon Him to His fate (He showed them the

highway with a flabby hand, and with the other He grabbed on to a trunk), to let Him rot on the marabou.

At night they'd take off His blanket and leave Him in the open—so that the night dew would cool his sores—in the light of the V of blinking headlights. In the morning they'd find Him softened, tearful, pecked at by birds.

They hiked down the Villa Clara hills. In the distance, streaking the pink fields, you could see the black lines of the railroad disappearing under the roofs of the kirshwasser factories, branching off on the other side, crossing the pine groves and fishing villages, or else following the rivers which swept along rafts of white trunks, convoyed by signal flags and toads, until disappearing into the curve of inlets, under the red smoke cloud of the distilleries, among the tanks along the docks.

Near a curve in the road they heard call bells. When they turned the corner, they saw two yellow triangles with red edges light up and a barrier fall before them: blocking the way, an armored train had stopped at the crossing.

The bell stopped. What a silence! (They felt they were being watched.) Suddenly the cars opened, unglued boxes, and down the walls, now ramps, tanks rolled out. From their turrets came nets full of green sponges ("Giant pieces of mint!"—Help), portable radios, tape recorders whose tapes were running.

"Somehow we've got to appeal to the popular devotion!"—declared Help, and she stamped the first letter on one buttock.

Let me explain: she was dancing in front of a jukebox, and wildly, pardon me, and enthusiastically composing the Lord's texts on her naked body—which looked as if printed on brown paper—: with wooden blocks she engraved golden monograms.

No one had come to receive them in Santa Clara. She tore her clothes in anger, crossed herself, and bought a printing set: (to Him):

> I will make of my body Your book,
> They will read from me!

And Mercy (*to the frightened Villa Clara folk behind cracks—families squeezed into bunches—hidden under their mothers' skirts*):

> Come, children of God:
> Here is the flesh made word!

And Help went wild over burning tambourines and cornets from John Coltrane's band.

They came running, and *en masse*. At the beat of the drums, Help wriggled from head to toe, and from her navel, which projected an O, to the full stop of her knee letters shined all over her.

He couldn't take His eyes off the oscillating band of texts, nor hold back His feet: He wanted to dance, He knew that dance is the new birth, that after death they'll confront us with the mambo band. What a pity! He couldn't even clap hands. He stretched His arms and felt like His armpits were breaking. He was finished now: His nipples were purple, His chest in welts, His throat burning, He was choking, the ganglia of His neck hurt. If the band came on louder—the needle in the striped grooves, for Him it was like bottles breaking against each other, cornets playing under water.

What wiggly hips!—(said the faithful). Bruno took some steps around her, looking at her hips as if reading.

"But, what about the helicopters? "

They were there. Watching the show from the boxes. The pilots eating popcorn. Whose bags they threw away when the record was over.

Let's not even talk about Matanzas.

THE ENTRY OF CHRIST IN HAVANA _____

What a reception in Havana! They were all waiting for Him. His picture was everywhere, endlessly repeated, to the point of ridicule or simply boredom: pasted up, ripped off, pulled apart, nailed on every door, pasted around every pole, decorated with mustaches, with pricks dripping into His mouth, even in colors—oh so blond and beautiful, just like Greta Garbo—not to mention the stained-glass reproductions in the Galiano subway. Wherever you look, He looks back.

BRUNO: I'm gonna walk no more: I'm sitting right down. I'm at my wit's end: They take more pictures of Him than of the Coca Cola bottle! Let somebody else carry Him. Here's where I'm staying.

And there he stayed, in a fit of hiccups.

Pictures, taken from above, but at different distances: a black spot, a winding line of the highway, tilled fields; a blond head, toes on a platform, a background of pavement, white locks, and up front His profile; close-up: His eyes. His eyes; white locks, profile; dark spot, highway.

A little black girl came running full steam ahead, with a banner waving in the breeze, white knee socks were all you could see of her tiny legs; she came running full steam ahead, her legs—pistons—were all over the place, her knees chugachugachuga—a Hittite lion—holding up high a banner that said INRI. You've finally come, she said, we were waiting for You. Her eyes became moist, she was speechless ("She swooned, in a trance, as if she had seen Paul Anka!"—said Help), she thrashed about wildly, out of joy, took a few steps toward Him, and fell.

He didn't have time to pick her up. Two others fell upon Him, more and more kept coming. Weeping and embracing Him. They came down from the hills, beating barrels and drums with sticks rolled up in rags. The women threw open their doors; dazed, they clapped their hands over their mouths; a cry; they dropped to their knees, tried to touch Him, kissed the ground where He passed. The children carried around His image in good luck charms, in little straw dolls. His name was in all the shop windows. They ate Him in mint candies. They dressed up like Him, wearing little crowns of thorns (their faces white with rice powder) and small blood flowers. It was all so pretty!

They came from every direction, climbed trees to see Him, asked for His autograph.

He coughed and suddenly felt that He was moving forward, the people pushing Him, that He was moving backward, driftwood floating in the tide, that He was moving forward again. Sweating. He had chills. They stepped on His feet. They blew their hot breath, thick fumes of Gold Label rum, into His face; the trumpets of Luyano in His ears. (The flutists were two jaundiced and baggy-eyed dwarfs, puffy cheeks under black berets.) He felt slimy hands caressing Him, and on His thighs wet mollusk lips. The banners covered His sky, the poles fenced Him in like a palisade of red lances. He was gasping for air. He thrashed His arms in acid fumes. He really wasn't made for the proletariat: the masses stifled Him.

"I'll never make it," He said to Himself. He tightened His eyes, clinched His fists, bit His lips. He wanted to stamp and kick. Spin around with His arms outstretched (and, God willing, with knives in both hands), open a path, escape. His dangling limbs did not obey Him. (Horns, rattles, bells) His hand shook as if it were throwing dice. He tried to stop it: one foot trembled, or was it the other or His head. His hand moved on its own. His feet. He jumped. His body quivered, a goaded frog. An electric shock ran through Him. He was dancing unwillingly to a rock beat. (Balloons popped out of a balcony, doves from another.)

He listened as if someone were whispering in His ear.. At the same time Help and Mercy turned toward Him. Once more (but the racket of brass bands, clapping, hur-rahs): stuttering, babbling words ("African angels are speaking to Me," He thought). Without turning His head, He looked in the direction of the voices. Attentive, He heard "red," and right after: "It hurts in the back of my eyes."

He saw Help and Mercy shake their heads, stand still, raise their open hands—restored to the fervor of the catacombs—turn from white to yellow and back again to white. Now two great tears rolled down their cheeks. Now they muttered, sobbing, "A miracle, a miracle."

Then He realized He was speaking.

He heard Himself say: "I am freezing inside."

They wrapped Him in the Madonna's cloak from the main altar in the Church of Carmen. The thick cloth, embroidered with gold leaves, hung straight down from His shoulders. Black cords intertwined in the shape of clover leaves and rosettes of pearls ran along its edges.

Each step of the bearers shook His blond head, his waxy eyelids, those sick eyes sank deeper. (From a distance He was the Madonna of a Siennese casket.) They threw flowers, they cheered Him. Without turning His head, with the solemnity of a princess in her Mercedes, He greeted the multitudes on the balconies. Carnations stuck to the garlands and brooches of His cloak.

"Blessed be ye, women, wise if not virgins, who have followed Me through thick and thin." He moved His forearm three times like a piggy-bank black boy who bows and doffs his cap. He suddenly unwound: His hands. They hung limp, like rags. He could not quite touch His eyelids:

"How cold they are, oh God, what a pain in the back of My eyes!" And they took off their cloaks, folded them like sashes, wrapped them around His waist. Or transported by mystical delirium ("May Your fire joyously consume me!"—said Help), they padded them, and with the same burlap filled in the gaps of His joints. They covered

His hinges. They would have torn out the pupils of their eyes to give Him. They wept with only one eye, so He would not see. They turned violet, their nails black, as if the Plague were devouring them.

(Thickness of the sky: terraces of wax.

And there, over the streets, the sea: fixed foam, a strip of sand.) He glided over the mob—carried on their shoulders—swift, blinded by the flash bulbs, followed by the cameras—concave green crossed the lenses—. Majestic, He was like a redwood statue unearthed from a river bed: His eyes sockets full of crabs, His face rotted, His arms broken, His feet black sponges. Branches and leaves of holy Palm trees opened before Him, like seaweed before the hull of a ship.

Posing in place, in order of generations, the families looked down at Him from their balconies. In the foreground, right behind the railing, little boys dressed in white suits and black bow ties, were rocking back and forth on their wooden horses, chocolate cigars between their fingers. Little girls, in starched dresses, held yellow hoops next to their perfectly conical skirts, beach pails, and shovels. Behind them, austere, the fathers with mustaches and goatees, and bouquets of flowers in their hands, the mothers in their fancy curls and bonnets, wrapped in shawls. And in the background, leaning against the doors, grinning at the photographer's birdie, the grandparents, gray-haired, almost dead.

The squares: theaters with identical boxes. A parade of toy horses, hoops, bouquets, toy horses.

Such repetition made Him dizzy, and the choruses too. Mercy touched His forehead with the back of her hand: It was burning. She pressed the wood and it crumbled. A white halo remaining. He had already rotted right through.

"King of the Four Roads, spare our sugar harvest!," shouted a reeling peasant with a bottle of rum in his hand, and he hung from Him, crying. Help tried to protect Him. But it was too late. The peasant had torn off a hand. A wooden stump remained, a splinter, out of which ants came scurrying.

The people came from all directions. They pushed. They squeezed together. It was a jungle of slender legs, knotty bamboo shoots supporting puffy buttocks, round like purple *caimitos*. Their trunks bent, swayed back, rocked by gusts of wind. In their midst, jumping over their wide feet, frightened black boys—little frogs—zigzagged around, fanning themselves.

A grandstand had been set up—with bleachers and platforms—and a red damask canopy hung over it, supported by four gilded halberds. Banners waved. Helicopters hovered above the square. From the platforms His followers threw them black balls which opened in midair: flowers of Chinese silk. They floated: black gardens. They fell; on the petals His name was imprinted: incomplete, backward, broken.

The sky was a crumpled piece of paper. A thick tent. Slow waves rolled through it: the ebb tide of a salty marsh. Something in the air was going to break.

"Come closer"—He said to them—"look at Me."

I am He who gives the Face. The big daddy-o. Mine is

the page of the Codex. Mine is the ink and the painted image. Where are you taking Me?

But an icy gust ripped open His cloak, tore down the flags.

The people trembled. They warmed each other with their breath. Their eyes were wide open. They murmured: "This is the day terror after death change rot House of the Black." They began to weep. They lowered their heads in prayer. They beat their brows. He heard Himself say: "Dear God, have pity on Me."

The families went inside: They closed the shutters. They bolted the doors. They piled up the furniture, and the children on top, against the doors so the wind would not blow them open. They covered the mirrors with sheets.

The storm raged. (The little black boys dropped their fans, clung to people's legs, buried their heads between their knees.) It grew dark. It was when they turned on the lights that they saw, in the lights' flickering cones, the white specks scrawling in the air, then orderly, with the slowness of stars, whirlwinds of sculptured water: it was snowing.

They huddled up under His cloak. They tried to warm Him "But He was already fucked up"—Help said—; and on to another prayer. The snow burned Him on the face, another kind of fever. He looked like a prisoner, a drowned man. His eyes were sunken and watery, the lids jaundiced, His lips oozing with pus, His neck bloated. Branches of black veins climbed to His throat. Knots of puffy ganglia, spongy animals, rotting between His bones and hide. When He coughed He felt something was burning inside.

When He spat, bloody water stained the handkerchief. He was scarcely breathing, sounding like an asthmatic sucking in air. Hunched over. Gasping. A fish on dry land.

"Come on, You're looking great. You look just like a Virgin of Charity!" (it's Mercy, to make Him happy)

Parallel furrows in the pavement. A carpet of ceiba flowers. White moss.

And He:

"Of all the spectacles I've seen, none…"

A fit of coughing broke His bronchial tubes. A downpour of snowflakes pelted Him ("Tiny bird feathers!"—said Help); the whirling propellers scattered them.

"If I should die upon the road, on my grave I want no flowers" (He said)—And He tried to smile, to reassure the last of the faithful. But when they beat the drums they sprayed needles of ice.

Smooth, a tin sky covered almost the whole landscape. Bell towers and the arms of windmills jutted out over the red roofs. Open bridges, beached ships run aground: the Almendares River multiplied them. Along the snowy banks, stained at intervals by scaffolds and cranes, dying fish were jumping. Sea gulls swooped down to peck at them.

He tightened His throat. He felt that something was bursting in His neck. A taste of copper, warm salt, came up. He spat blood.

He was now a gargoyle, a snow white rag. Help, in a fit of tears, passed her hand over His head, dried the sweat from His brow, murmured in His ear, "It will soon be over, have faith, it will soon be over." And Mercy, in a fit of tears, patted Him on the back, kissed His temples, murmured in His ear: "It will soon be over, have faith, it will soon be over."

The snow slanted down. At the eaves, broken spirals, veins of white ink that He saw erased, with each gust of wind, to reappear, each time wider.

In the depths of their sockets, His eyes grew glassy. He did not move them. Help and Mercy dragged Him a few steps; they looked at each other: they turned to shout. His body shook. He was weeping. And when He calmed down:

"Why all this moaning?"—He said—. "Kicking the bucket is great fun. Life only begins after death, the life."

He was choking.

Cutting through the snow, a coach sped by.

Like zinc, from afar, the Havana lakes. Small covered bridges crossed them. On the shore there were austere towers of fortresses, palaces of cedar, tall dove cotes amidst cherry orchards, the ruins of synagogues, cut off minarets: there Infanta Street, frozen, crosses San Lázaro.

"Let's go, every man for himself!"—He heard them shout. He tried to raise His head. Then He saw the grandstand crushed by an avalanche. "Oh God"—He moaned—"Why didn't You throw in the towel?" The faithful left the square in groups, under yellow raincoats held over themselves with raised arms. The leaders carried lanterns. Helicopters spotlighted them with their floodlights: dotted lines.

"Who has stayed behind?"—(poor thing!)

And They:

"Loyal Ones, Followers, Shadows."

On the façades of colonial palaces the snow covered capitals, moldings, cement flowers. Closed gates; the blue shadow of the latches extended over the iron. Only half-moons, contorted masks, remained of the medallions with the heads of viceroys. Squirrels fled across the cornices.

Sunken gardens. Silent fountains: the tritons driveled threads of ice.

"Curtains of bread crumbs" (said Help).

"Who up there is shaking His tablecloth?" (said Mercy). One of His hands came loose. Swollen, it fell to the ground; in its palm, a sore.

It stayed there, for a moment, on the white cloth; purple knuckles. Three red drops fell upon it, from the wrist, it was buried by the snow.

The Entry of Christ into Death

He saw quick reddish stains in the snow, copper shadows. The ground moved away from Him. He was losing footing. He felt He was entering another space. Burning zone, He heard water through swollen leaves, the sleep of rattlesnakes and birds, the ambush. Behind vines, the frightened flight of mockingbirds. Cascades of moss, thick dark green mats, fell from the highest fronds, clouding the day. Light tigers carried bleeding ducks in their teeth. He heard His steps in the mud, on damp leaves. With the sound of water among rocks, the strokes of a guitar reached His ear. Then the drums, yes: it was the mambo band, the one that greets us on the other side.

His body became strange to Him: a pile of rotting sticks under the snow. Help and Mercy closed His eyes. He saw himself twisted, a broken gargoyle.

Meanwhile, He crossed reverberating forests, stockades of sugar cane that ended in golden leaves. He was getting close. Already among the sputtering sparks of flowers you could see the musicians. He knew that He was going to dance. That dancing means meeting the Dead.

That if you dance well, you get in.

He saw himself crumble. He fell into pieces, with a moan. Wood falling in water. His bald, leprous head split in two. The empty holes of the eyes, the white, perforated lips, the nose in its bone, the ears plugged with two black clots. And further on, the forehead, the cold globes of the eyes, the trunk, with an arm that sank into the snow as if looking for something buried. And further up, the curve of the back. The legs in pieces; the snow buried them.

And the foot that stamped three times, the belch, the first beat. He jumped. Two more steps, two steps. He clapped hands to the rhythm. He did a turn. Holding a white handkerchief. He danced on one foot. The band players shook their little bells near His ear. "Who can beat Me?"—He said to Himself. And He wiggled His hips. The musicians gathered around Him. Twice they suddenly changed the batá beat of the tambourines and twice He caught up to them with a caper. He was blond and handsome. And had white feet. He whirled around. Then the other way. Superimposed on Himself. He was blond. He was naked.

Holding a white handkerchief. He shouted again. "Sugar!"—they shouted to Him. He laughed. He wore gold bracelets. Not as shiny as His eyes.

He didn't know that the snow had stopped. Rivulets of mud cracked the white cloth, creased it at the sewers. It was sunny. Grating rails and throwing off sparks, the trolleys, full, passed by again. The river ran. The ships cast off.

(In the parks the old men chatted.)

Then the Faithful, the Fates, crossed the square. They started picking Him up, searching in the mire. Piece by piece, they wrapped Him in a cloth with loving care. They hurried away.

They were already reaching the portals when, from the helicopters, bullets rained down.

Note: Three cultures, at least, have been superimposed to constitute the Cuban—Spanish, African, and Chinese—; three fictions alluding to them constitute this book.

These fables share in common three characters—or themes—: Mortal, the blond Spaniard whose Castillian is spotless and who possesses the always uncertain attributes of power; Help and Mercy, also called the Flower Girls, the Ever Present, the Siamese Twins, the Divine Ones, the Thirsty Ones, the Majas...the Fates. (A third sister, Clemency, accidentally joins them.)

In the first narrative—*By the River of Rose Ashes*—Mortal Perez is a lecherous old general who pursues the image of Lotus Flower, a soprano—he thinks—at the Chinatown Opera House. Here everything is looking, contemplation, evanescent reality. If Lotus Flower really is a paint-smeared fraud, Help and Mercy are gifted with (and abuse) the power of metamorphosis: chorus girls at the Opera, and two-bit whores, they will make their heads, armored arms and legs proliferate, to frighten the general—A Siviac Band—. This will be light, the absence of light. In a *café-concert* they will coexist with their own mutations. "Grass"—hashish—and "white sugar"—cocaine—which Dragon Puss distributes, haunt this space of symmetrical arts: Painting and Torture.

In *Dolores Rondón,* Mortal is only a politician of emphatic oratory in his stages of councilman, candidate to the Senate, senator and ex-senator. But these ups and downs mark the life of Dolores Rondón, a Camagüeyan mulatto. This story—sound, action: theater—spells out a ten-line poem engraved on a tombstone in a Camagüey cemetery. Her only work, Dolores Rondón wrote it as an epitaph. The one-act farce, in ten "moments," respects the order of the lines (not the chronological) and the demands of its genre.

In *The Entry of Christ in Havana* Mortal is an absent young lover who is going to become a metaphor of Christ. Help and Mercy search for him; the desire for Mortal that ails them will turn into a thirst for eternal life. Here the two women will illustrate two main currents of Hispanic culture—Faith and Experience in the tapestry—opposites which polarize the continuous turns of the text: if the beginning evokes a certain pompousness, Zurbarán, soon the *vanities,* Valdes Leal, will appear; if Mercy quixotizes, Help is a Sancho Panza collection of proverbs. With a wooden Christ and Bruno—the Prince and his guest, Hiccups, in the tapestry—both will go on a pilgrimage through Cuba. The corruption of that wood corresponds to the corruption of time, and context: growing anachronisms, other landscapes superimposed on the Cuban, the reiteration and unreality of snow.

Curriculum Cubense introduces the characters. Help behaves awkwardly in the Self-Service; the delirious description of her photographs, which she hands out to all present, is not enough to impose another image of her. As for Mercy, she comes back frustrated from her visit to the House of God. In the Domus Dei, the one she searches for is "conspicuous for her absence." Both want to disappear, to be someone else: therefore the constant transformation, the wealth of cosmetics, artifices.

The general desires Lotus Flower; Dolores desires power; Help and Mercy, the body of a man, the soul's salvation. This man is the same, those worlds attract, will unite, reflect each other: in the midst of the Sivaic Band a Yoruba altar appears, in Christ's reception in Havana, Chinese decorations. Dolores's monologues emphasize this mirror quality. Among its constant figures throughout the centuries, Rhetoric has catalogued the *excusatio propter infirmitatem,* that confession of modesty, of incapacity before the theme to be developed, that must precede all discourse. I don't use it here (although denial is one of its forms): the impertinence of the preceding pages declares it for me, more than enough.

SEVERO SARDUY

Severo Sarduy (b. 1937), an important and versatile avantgarde Cuban novelist, poet, playwright, essayist, and painter, lived in Paris from 1960 until his death in June 1993, of AIDS. His works in English include *From Cuba with a Song* (1966; reissued by Sun & Moon Press, 1994), *Cobra* (1972; reissued by Dalkey Archive Press, 1995) and *Maitreya* (1978; reissued by Dalkey Archive Press, 1995), translated by Suzanne Jill Levine. *Escrito sobre un cuerpo* (1969), his first book of essays, has been translated by Carol Maier in a collection (including later essays) titled *Written on a Body* (Lumen Books, 1989), and Philip Barnard translated *For Voice*, four radio plays (*Para la voz*, 1977; Latin American Literary Press, 1985). *Christ on the Rue Jacob* (in a translation by Suzanne Jill Levine and Carol Maier) will be published by Mercury House.

SUZANNE JILL LEVINE

Suzanne Jill Levine, a professor at the University of California, Santa Barbara, is a distinguished and prolific translator of the most innovative writers from Latin America, and author of *The Subversive Scribe: Translating Latin American Fiction* (1991). She is currently working on a biography of Manuel Puig.

SUN & MOON CLASSICS

This publication was made possible, in part, through an operational grant from the Andrew W. Mellon Foundation and through contributions from the following individuals:

Charles Altieri (Seattle, Washington)
John Arden (Galway, Ireland)
Jesse Huntley Ausubel (New York, New York)
Dennis Barone (West Hartford, Connecticut)
Jonathan Baumbach (Brooklyn, New York)
Guy Bennett (Los Angeles, California)
Bill Berkson (Bolinas, California)
Steve Benson (Berkeley, California)
Charles Bernstein and Susan Bee (New York, New York)
Dorothy Bilik (Silver Spring, Maryland)
José Camillo Cela (in memorium)
Bill Corbett (Boston, Massachusetts)
Fielding Dawson (New York, New York)
Robert Crosson (Los Angeles, California)
Tina Darragh and P. Inman (Greenbelt, Maryland)
Christopher Dewdney (Toronto, Canada)
George Economou (Norman, Oklahoma)
Elaine Equi and Jerome Sala (New York, New York)
Lawrence Ferlinghetti (San Francisco, California)
Richard Foreman (New York, New York)
Howard N. Fox (Los Angeles, California)
Jerry Fox (Aventura, Florida)
In Memoriam: Rose Fox
Melvyn Freilicher (San Diego, California)
Miro Gavran (Zagreb, Croatia)
Peter Glassgold (Brooklyn, New York)
Barbara Guest (New York, New York)
Perla and Amiram V. Karney (Bel Air, California)
Fred Haines (Los Angeles, California)
Václav Havel (Prague, The Czech Republic)
Fanny Howe (La Jolla, California)
Harold Jaffe (San Diego, California)
Ira S. Jaffe (Albuquerque, New Mexico)
Alex Katz (New York, New York)
Tom LaFarge (New York, New York)
Mary Jane Lafferty (Los Angeles, California)

Michael Lally (Santa Monica, California)
Norman Lavers (Jonesboro, Arkansas)
Jerome Lawrence (Malibu, California)
Stacey Levine (Seattle, Washington)
Herbert Lust (Greenwich, Connecticut)
Norman MacAffee (New York, New York)
Rosemary Macchiavelli (Washington, DC)
Beatrice Manley (Los Angeles, California)
Martin Nakell (Los Angeles, California)
Toby Olson (Philadelphia, Pennsylvania)
Maggie O'Sullivan (Hebden Bridge, England)
Rochelle Owens (Norman, Oklahoma)
Marjorie and Joseph Perloff (Pacific Palisades, California)
Dennis Phillips (Los Angeles, California)
Carl Rakosi (San Francisco, California)
David Reed (New York, New York)
Ishmael Reed (Oakland, California)
Janet Rodney (Santa Fe, New Mexico)
Joe Ross (Washington, DC)
Dr. Marvin and Ruth Sackner (Miami Beach, Florida)
Floyd Salas (Berkeley, California)
Tom Savage (New York, New York)
Leslie Scalapino (Oakland, California)
James Sherry (New York, New York)
Aaron Shurin (San Francisco, California)
Charles Simic (Strafford, New Hampshire)
Gilbert Sorrentino (Stanford, California)
Catharine R. Stimpson (Staten Island, New York)
John Taggart (Newburg, Pennsylvania)
Nathaniel Tarn (Tesuque, New Mexico)
Fiona Templeton (New York, New York)
Mitch Tuchman (Los Angeles, California)
Hannah Walker and Ceacil Eisner (Orlando, Florida)
Wendy Walker (New York, New York)
Anne Walter (Carnac, France)
Arnold Wesker (Hay on Wye, England)

If you would like to be a contributor to this series, please send your tax-deductible contribution to The Contemporary Arts Educational Project, Inc., a nonprofit corporation, 6026 Wilshire Boulevard,Los Angeles, California 90036.

*First American publication
**Revised edition